At last the bounteous feast came to an end and our full stomachs craved a rest. While we were reclining on our divans, our host clapped his hands.

In response to this signal the embroidered curtains were thrust aside and two lovely Geishas entered with graceful step. Their only covering was their long black hair.

They were scarcely seventeen years of age, and lovely beyond description. Their forms were the perfection of beauty – their ripe bosoms were distracting to behold and their shapely thighs would have made a sculptor envious.

As we watched in lustful silence, the two girls took the first steps of their sensual dance . . .

Also available from Headline:

Eros in the Country
Eros in the Town
Eros on the Grand Tour
Eros in the New World
Venus in Paris
A Lady of Quality
Sweet Fanny
Sweet Fanny's Diary
The Love Pagoda
The Education of a Maiden
Maid's Night In
Lena's Story
Lord Hornington's Academy of Love
Cremorne Gardens
The Lusts of the Borgias

States of Ecstasy

Two Erotic Stories from the Victorian Era

Anonymous

HEADLINE

Copyright © 1990 Headline Book Publishing PLC

First published in 1990
by HEADLINE BOOK PUBLISHING PLC

10 9 8 7 6 5 4 3

All rights reserved. No part of this publication may be
reproduced, stored in a retrieval system, or transmitted,
in any form or by any means without the prior written
permission of the publisher, nor be otherwise circulated
in any form of binding or cover other than that in which
it is published and without a similar condition being
imposed on the subsequent purchaser.

All characters in this publication are fictitious
and any resemblance to real persons, living or dead,
is purely coincidental.

ISBN 0 7472 3437 X

Typeset in 10/12¼ pt English Times
by Colset Private Limited, Singapore

Printed and bound in Great Britain by
Collins, Glasgow

HEADLINE BOOK PUBLISHING PLC
Headline House,
79 Great Titchfield Street
London W1P 7FN

CONTENTS

**THE AMOROUS ADVENTURES OF A
JAPANESE GENTLEMAN**   1

BLIND LUST   113

The Amorous Adventures of a Japanese Gentleman

INTRODUCTORY

Early in the Spring of ninety-one we put in at Yokohama, according to our orders, to coal and take on supplies. A number of our men were granted shore-leave, among whom was the writer of these introductory pages. Having drawn some money from the purser, we put off, as one of our party expressed it, for a little cruise about town.

For several hours we wandered about the streets. Everything appeared so strange and novel to us that we could not help gazing; and I am afraid more than one swarthy Japanese beauty as she clattered by on high wooden shoes, must have felt somewhat abashed at our bold and almost rude glances. As Ensign, I naturally kept alongside the Lieutenant, and both of us were equally observing of women and things. For my part, mine was curiosity, while his gaze, I noted more than once, was bold and inviting. Our American women would have resented his insults; but many of the Japanese beauties merely laughed in our faces. Thus we spent the afternoon till almost sundown.

Tired, at length, of sight-seeing, and of jostling among the motley crowd, Lieutenant Harris as the head of our party, proposed a trip across the river among the tea-houses.

'But I don't like tea,' I objected.

'I do,' returned the Lieutenant, 'the kind they have here

is a big T – tail, cunt – which ever you choose to call it.'

'That's the kind they have there – and lots of it too,' said an old salt, who was with us.

'Would you like to go, Ned?' asked the Lieutenant.

The old salt saluted.

'If your honours would permit, I could show you some mighty tall sights.'

'Can you screw, Ned?' asked the Lieutenant, chaffingly.

'Like a bull, sir,' was the prompt reply.

'Then you're just the man for us. Lead the way, Ned, and we'll follow. You're Captain. Now, lead off.'

We walked for some little distance, hailed a jinrikisha driver, and were taken in his cart across the bridge.

'Mr Budd,' said old Ned, turning to me, 'did you ever have a piece of a Japanese woman?'

'Why no, Ned – this is my first trip.'

'Well, Mr Budd, they're fine. You only want to know one Jap word to get along with them. Put your arm round her neck and say *skibi*, and you can do what you will with her.'

Presently a house, then another, and still another came into the view. Each had a large pole in front of it, or over the doorway, just as barber shops in our own country use a striped pole as a sign. I asked Ned what it meant.

'What does it look like?' asked Ned.

'By George! It looks like a human tool – a penis in fact,' vowed Lieutenant Harris.

'That's what it means,' said Ned. 'That's a skibi-pole – it's the sign of a house of accommodation. Shall we go there, or further on to the tea-houses?'

'The tea-houses by all means,' said the Lieutenant, as others of our party came up.

A few moments more brought us to one which Ned said was the finest place in town.

INTRODUCTORY

The Lieutenant counted noses.

'Thirteen!' he said, 'Unlucky. Let's find some one to make it up. Ah! Here comes a man. Ned, ask him to come with us.'

Ned stepped up to a gorgeously apparelled Japanese gentleman, who was coming towards us in his jinrikisha. After a few words of colloquy he dismounted and stood smiling and bowing before us.

'Gentlemen,' said Ned, 'this is our new friend, Mr Hoyo – I forget the rest.'

'Hoyo, Ishitura Nanhomu, Daimio of Satsuma,' replied the newcomer.

Ned explained matters a little further, and then we turned to the tea-house.

'Come on, boys!' said the Lieutenant, and we entered.

It was a large apartment, sheltered by a porch. In front, near the doorway, reclined as handsome a Japanese woman as I ever saw. She was drinking tea, but set down the cup as we came up, and rising, bowed to the very ground before us.

'Lords, welcome,' she said. Then she led us into the large apartment, and closed the screen door. The woman, seeing our party arranged in a row along one side of the room, blew a shrill whistle. Immediately servants entered with rice cakes, saki and tea. When we had taken our places, and had accepted of the refreshments offered us, a door in one corner opened, and some forty women, of various ages, entered and filed round the room before us. We were told to choose from among them. This having been done, the selected ones each stood beside her chosen lord and the rest retired, without a word, or even a look. Nor did we see them afterwards. They vanished as noiselessly as so many ghosts.

Ned collected our money, and taxed us each a silver

dollar. This money he turned over to the mistress of the place – whom by the way he had selected for himself. My choice was a young girl, light and lithe of figure – whom I could recall only as wearing a bright red flower, amid her dark luxuriant tresses.

The room now being cleared of all save what you might call the active couples, the women left us with sundry bows.

My partner gave me a soft kiss, pressing against my lips the tip of her little red tongue, and left to join the rest. They stood in the centre of the room, formed a group or ring, and then began to pose.

From somewhere – some concealed alcove perhaps – came soft strains of music, a Japanese melody, which as soon as our ears got accustomed to its peculiarities, no longer sounded harsh or discordant; and then the group of girls began a dance.

They place themselves in a variety of the most lascivious positions. First they pose as if inviting us to enjoy all their charms; the next moment they seem to be coy and retiring. Now a dainty ankle is shown; now a lovely brown breast, with sweet little strawberry nipples, displayed.

Presently one of the dancers slips. In an instant her clothing is stripped from her, and she lies sprawling upon the floor, panting, but beaming with merriment and naked as the day she was born. What a lovely sight she presents! Instinctively my tool springs up, erect, and so eager for action that it throbs and palpitates against my pants in amorous agony.

Now the dance continues. It grows even more voluptuous. Another dancer slips or makes a mistake, and loses her clothes as a penalty. And now the brown bottoms, plump thighs, finely developed calves, and red-lipped, olive-tinged slits present themselves before us and lash us into love's most furious frenzy.

INTRODUCTORY

And so it continues till but two remain. One lifts up the other's clothes, displaying a most beautifully rounded bum, and brings her hand down upon it with a slap that resounds through the apartment, and awakens peals of rippling laughter, as well as shouts from the men. The daring one is my little girl with the red flower.

The other chases her. My partner runs to me. But the rest of the spectators desire to see the fun, and so I am not permitted to protect her.

So in and out they go among us, until my little girl trips over a prostrate nude figure, and falls. The other with one fierce clutch divests her of her garments, and exposes all her charms to my eager and gloating eyes. Then with her open palm she returns the slap with such force as to leave the red print of her hand upon the delicate skin of my chosen one.

But the girl with the red flower is not down long. She grasps a stick some ten inches in length a skibistick, as Ned explains it a sort of wooden dildoe. Armed with this, she gives chase to her late pursuer.

Again they fairly fly around the room. In and out they go among our crowd. As she passes, her tempting slit comes so close to me that I noticed that it is as hairless as a babe's. The very sight of it sets me frantic with desire. She is gone, but not without having given me a glance that foretells coming joys.

As the pursued one comes close to Ned, the old salt, actuated by some sudden impulse, makes a grab at the girl's clothes as she passes; there is a rip, and she, too, is stark naked.

My partner, panting and almost breathless, pursues her. The excitement of the chase has made them rosy and glowing. She gains upon her – she deftly trips her with a swift movement of her dainty little foot. Like a flash she is kneeling on the other. She turns her rival over on her back, and amid our shouts and shrieks of laughter buries the ten inch skibi-stick deep in the other's grotto of love and works it vigorously. Back and forth, in and out, faster and faster, does she pump away at the now thoroughly alarmed and excited girl, until at length comes the climax. Her arms relax, her eyes roll, and the frothy cream begins to rise to the surface.

Then as if tiring of the sport, she leaves and quickly runs to my side. As she crosses the room she deftly dodges the skibi-stick, which the other girl has sent flying after her.

This is the signal for the others. They rejoin their partners, and in a few moments the screens against the wall are pulled out and adjusted. The large room is now divided into about fifteen smaller ones. Each girl goes out, but returns bringing a quilt from a closet in the adjoining room. This being placed on the floor is to serve as our bed, and then every couple retires to devote themselves to the gratification of that passion which has been wrought in each to the highest pitch.

My partner's passions and my own were now intensely excited. Oh! What a feast was before me! I could not speak in words, but here even actions were eloquent with meaning. I know mine were.

She stood teasingly before me. The little angel was the very picture of love. Her pretty eyes sparkled and glowed with the flames of awakened passion and kindled desire. The sweet little rosebud of a mouth uttered plaintive language in a tongue unknown to me. Her lithesome body swayed forward and backward as if a swelling penis were already encased lovingly in the enticing little hairless slit. Oh! How I longed to kiss its jutting lips. See – it quivers, it palpitates, it opens. God! Can I stand it any more?

INTRODUCTORY

Oh! What a lovely little slit it was! The olive-tinted skin made the red-lipped grotto all the more prominent. Not a hair shaded it. No curling chevelure was there to hide beauties from me. I gazed with all my eyes. Mine, all mine! I threw myself at her feet, seeking to grasp her loins, thinking thus to bring the lovely lips of her gate of paradise to my lips for a long amorous kiss. Like a frightened fawn, it fled from me, her plump arse still moving to and fro – now slow, now fast, and faster yet. She stirred not a foot, yet her body moved with astonishing speed. Every time she made a forward movement, the hairless slit was within a foot of me.

I held out my arms appealingly. My staff was painful in its stiffness. Then I disrobed rapidly. The little teaser, with her head thrown to one side, parted her lips in a grin and displayed a mouth full of pearls, and critically inspected my every procedure. In a moment more I had completely undressed. I was now as naked as herself.

Though the space allotted to us was quite small, yet I could not, for some little time, succeed in imprisoning my charmer. Finally I grasped her thighs. She ceased struggling. With a cry of joy I pressed my lips to the font of love. I kissed it a hundred times in as many seconds, she meanwhile grasping my penis in her little hand, working it as if it were hinged.

Then I threw her over on the cushions which she had deftly arranged so as to bring her slit uppermost. With a cry of delight I fell upon her and, joining my lips to her own, commenced to enjoy the most entrancing screw I had ever tasted. Her slit was like a vice. When the head of my penis entered her, she closed upon it and held me there for a moment then, clasping both arms and legs about me, she held me in that position. Her warm breath fanned my cheek. I could feel her breasts throbbing against my chest in amorous bliss. They rose and fell, rose and fell, and it seemed to me that each nipple titillated itself against me, like a miniature penis.

Then she spoke. She did not command much English, but made herself understood.

'Me Yone,' she said. 'How you?'

'My name's Walter,' I answered, kissing her.

'Yone no speak much English,' she said.

Then she slipped one hand down between our bodies, causing an electric thrill of pleasure wherever she touched me. It rested upon my penis, in loving caressing grasp.

'Good skibi!' she said, 'Yone like good big skibi. Yone's cunt speak good English, Walter?' – this with sundry coaxing kisses.

'Yes, Yone,' I replied.

Immediately the vice-like grip in which my penis had been held was loosened, and Yone's hand was removed. I began to enter the portals of paradise with a slow even progress, the road being yielded with a pleasant gentleness that prolonged the delight, which she seemed to most keenly enjoy. Yes, Yone's cunt spoke most eloquent English. For as old Ned had often quoted me from *his* copy of *Don Juan* (he will swear to its reading so),

> The language of fucking's so well understood,
> That even a savage can speak it quite good.

Oh! How I fucked her! I was delirious with the maddening joy. Yone wriggled beneath me, and set me off on a rattling pace. My arse began to move quickly. My strokes came as fast as those of the piston-rod of an engine only my piston-rod had the electric energy of pleasure behind it.

INTRODUCTORY

'What a splendid cunt you have, Yone!' I shouted. 'And you know how to use it – Oh! You fuck fine! – Oh! Jesus! I am going to squirt!'

I was quite oblivious of the fact that the little beauty did not quite understand me. But she knew the word fuck right well. She rolled her black eyes till only the whites could be seen, and gurgled 'Fuck! Fuck! Fuck! – He! – He! – Me know fuck! Good fuck!'

I pressed my lips to hers. I fairly glued them there. Our hot breaths intermingled. Then something warmer touched my lips, it passed them and twined itself about my tongue. In short our tongues began to play fast and loose with one another. Then I grasped tight hold of her plump little arse. She gave a sudden shove that buried me deeper in her than I had yet been, and withdrew her lips from mine with a long sigh of mingled pleasure and amorous satisfaction. Her legs gripped mine as in a vice. With the plump cheeks of her backside tightly grasped in my hands I strained her closer to me, and cried out.

'Here I come! – Yes! Yes! – I come! – Take it, you little devil! – Whoop! Now I'm off!'

Yone squirmed and wriggled like a snake, as my charge entered her. But my tool still remained hard, and I kept on working. The pent up flood of her passion came pouring down, but seemed only to lubricate rod and box to better working.

'Fuck! Fuck! Fuck!' she cried.

As she said this she rolled me over and over with such force that we struck the light screen on one side. Down it went, and the next scene that met my view was most amusing.

It chanced that the Daimio of Satsuma was my neighbour. He had for a partner, a little angel of some sixteen or seventeen summers, she was mounted in a sitting position upon his cock, and he was playing horse with her. Without pausing, he gave the light screen a kick, and uttered a jangle of Japanese oaths that made Yone shudder as with a sudden chill. Then he laid his partner down and pumped rapidly with his arse. But before coming, he jumped up. He pranced around like a wild horse, his big fat thighs standing out like two small pillows.

'Fuck! Fuck! Fuck!' Yone cries. 'Me! Me! Me!'

But I was fucked out. My John Thomas had shot its load again. That settled me for a short period.

In the meantime, the Daimio was acting like one possessed. He would lay his partner on the floor, and pump away at her furiously. Then he would jump up and kick around like a *danseuse*. Then his face began to assume a variety of expressions. He gritted his teeth. His eyes bulged out, then back. His mouth opened. His partner was licking his lips and face. Down they got on the floor. His arse moved convulsively. This called forth a remark from my partner, who had been watching them attentively.

'Him squirtee now,' said Yone. 'Me know him. Fuck good – good.'

The girl had evidently been in his company.

The Daimio's arse was now still.

'Him squirtee much,' continued Yone. 'Squirtee much – much. Melican no squirtee like Jap.'

It was evident that she was right. I could see by the expression on the face of the Daimio's girl that she was greatly pleased. She kept licking her partner's face every time it came close to her. It was plain to be seen that the Japanese gentleman could fuck like a stud-horse.

Suddenly a shout came from the Daimio. It was evidently a command. Hardly had he uttered it than every screen in the large apartment was drawn up to the ceiling.

Oh! Goddess of Love! What a sight! Naked forms were in motion all about me. The men seemed greatly put out, but the women showed by their shouts of laughter that the scene was not new to them.

Right next to me a tempting morsel of womanhood was moulding her partner's tool. She uttered little cries of 'He! He! He!' Every now and then she stopped to kiss its crimson head. Now she would push down its foreskin. Then both hands would work it up. Next it would be placed in her lovely hairless slit. Then she would draw it out, rub it with her fingers and kiss it repeatedly.

My partner was not long in following suit. She took my diminished penis in her hand, and began the same kind of fondling motions. The most delightful sensations pierced me. Never did I enjoy such pleasures.

Fucking, kissing, manipulating were going on all about me. The women acted as though crazed with venery.

'Ha! What think you now?' cried the Daimio. 'I have been to your America – but give me Japan, and I die happy. You should see us in Mikao,' he continued, his hand all the while working in his partner's slit, while she was fondling his bull-headed tool. 'Yes, in Mikao,' he repeated. 'We have fifty thousand public women there. They are said to to be the finest fuckers in the world.'

He was interrupted by a loud shriek. A naked Venus was rushing around the room. Every time she saw a prick she fell upon it, and stroked and kissed it a dozen times.

'Melican's good fuck!' she cried as she came to me. 'But skibi not as thick as Jap. Jap skibi squirtee plentee juicee. Melican skibi not much juicee.'

As she said this, she grasped the Daimio's tool and spoke Japanese words of love to it.

But she was not by him long. His partner pushed her way.

'She's on the rampage,' said Lieutenant Harris, who had a small tid-bit of a Japanese woman. 'Look out for her, boys. She bites!'

'By God! Boys,' shouts the old salt. 'She nearly took a piece out of my cock!'

The mistress of the house, who was Ned's partner, said something in her own language. The girl at once subsided.

Once more we turned to our partners. Every cock in the room stood erect. We were all ready for another battle.

Again the Daimio was prancing round. This was evidently his favourite method.

Yone could not wait. She fairly pushed my tool into her. I lunged. Now I played with her. I put my prick in to the full. Then I found room to play with her clitoris. As I pulled my tool out I put my finger in, and rubbed her quickly. This touched her to the quick. Her legs thrown up, wildly kicking in the air.

'By God!' I cried 'if that don't suit you, nothing will.'

'He! – He! – He! Fuck! – Fuck! – Fuck!' she exclaimed.

'Who wouldn't?' said I. 'This is just great! – How are you doing, Lieutenant?' I inquired, as looking in his direction, I saw him lying underneath his partner, his prick encased in her slit.

He was slapping her olive-tinged arse with vigorous blows.

'Don't it take the cake!' he replies. 'This is the best thing, Walt, that I have ever had. It is worth a year's cruise to get into a slit like this. Oh! It is too fine! – Oh! You angel, take that! Oh! By God! I could eat you! – That's right! Work your arse like hell! Work it! Work it! I'll give you a squirt soon that will make you jump!'

A grunt from the corner, caused me to look up. I saw old Ned.

'How goes it, old boy!' I shouted over to him.

'I'm getting fucked out,' he answered, a little dolorously. 'This is an old cow that I have got. I gave it to her three times, and now she squeals for more. Say, boys, who wants to change. My cock don't fit.'

Not a soul offered to change. Ned had only himself to blame, for he had been offered a fine young thing, but took the mistress in preference.

'You see, boys,' he remarked, 'I haven't had a fuck for a year, and no young unbroken thing will do. I want one well-broken in.'

He had got what he wanted and we all thought he ought to be made to stick to his decision.

Meanwhile I had not been idle. Yone's soft hand was playing around my backside. It gripped my bag of cream, and pressed it as if to force me to spend. But I was slow in coming. So were all the rest of the men. Yone had covered my tool with her emission, as my titillation of her clitoris excited her to the highest pitch. Her slit was soft and smooth as velvet. I removed my finger and commenced to work vigorously. With a soft sigh of pleasure, her hand relaxed its grip, and I was free. Still I kept pushing it into her. My strokes were slow, firm, and deliberate. The keenness of the pleasure made her fairly squirm again.

All around me I heard shouts and cries of joy. English and Japanese intermingled, created a very babel of sounds.

The Daimio had risen, with his partner impaled on his strong stiff tool. He had run to the wall with her, and was vigorously pushing her arse against it. He was right before me, the very muscles on his back stood out like whip-cords. He kept this up for a short time. Then he fell on the floor, she on top of him. His hands were still pressed on her young arse.

I had little or no time for them, however.

'I am going off again!' I shouted.

'He! He! He! – Fuck! Fuck! Fuck!' cried Yone.

Then I let go. Whoop de dooden do! But didn't I pour it in! The woman grasped me convulsively. She has lost possession of her senses. She dug her fingers deep into my flesh. She tightened her grip upon me. She hugged herself so close to me that I could scarcely stir. She licked my face. God! I could scarcely breathe! Her strength was greater than mine. I sought to loose myself. At first my effort only made her grip me tighter. I tried to release myself from her clasp. She would not have it so. I felt my tool rapping against the very top of her womb. It dwindled. I could feel its stiffness departing. She heaved sigh after sigh of pleasure. Her arms relaxed a little, and so finally I succeed in mastering her. Her eyes closed. She gave a gasp as if dying, and lay on the floor like a log.

'Ha! Boy, this is fucking!' cried the Lieutenant. 'The Japs have got their screwing down to a fine art!'

Saying this he reached for his uniform and took from the pocket half a dozen new silver dollars. He threw them into the air. As they fell to the floor, the women made a dash for them. The lively scramble that ensued made us nearly die with laughter. The sight of the named women piling on top of one another in their eagerness to get a coin was worth going a thousand miles to see.

I threw a handful of dollars in another part of the room. Again the scramble, the shrieks, and exclamations; the quaint poses, and odd grimaces that made our very sides ache with laughter. Others followed my example. The screams recalled Yone to her senses.

Meanwhile Ned's companion, the mistress of the house, became wild with rage. Though she had taxed us before we had entered the room, yet she was not satisfied. With shrieks and gestures she ordered the girls to hand the money over to her. But Lieutenant Harris would not permit it.

'We want to pay those girls for the sweet pleasure their bodies have given us – don't we, boys?' he cried.

We all shouted in the affirmative, so fiercely that the woman was terrified into quietness.

The girls by their actions showed their gratitude. Every one knelt at her partner's feet, and kissed the fallen pricks that had so ably battled for pleasure.

The men were not to be outdone. They knelt and kissed the beautiful hairless slits in front of them. Then the women, as a further token, began a voluptuous Hutchi-Kutchi dance.

By Heaven! It was a splendid sight! The dance illustrated the progress of the art of love. Now the breasts thrust forward, then the stomachs. Next the hairless slits. Every action indicated desire. The loins sprang backward at first, with a slow motion. Then as the sexual agony is supposed to increase, the action became quicker.

The variety of slits before us was numerous. Some had pouting red lips, very prominent. Others had soft lines to mark the little orifice which man so madly worships. Some showed decided marks of wear; others not the slightest effects of use.

Now see! Their motions quicken. With one accord they work their arses furiously. The crisis is approaching. The spending period has arrived. Short, quick, vigorous motions indicate that the seed is being planted to produce new life. Then as a finale the motions are slow. The seed has been received. The after pleasure is too exquisite for furious action. Gentle heaves indicate the extremes of bliss.

This finished the performance. At its conclusion the girls retired. They returned to serve us a cup of saki and some cakes. And then kissing us a farewell, they left the room.

'I say, boys,' shouted old Ned, as we were dressing, 'the man who is not thankful to God for his prick deserves to burn in hell for ten thousand years.'

The dawn was just beginning to break as we left the tea-house. The rosy fingers of Eros had already streaked the east as we approached the town proper, and by the time we reached ship-board, the reddening sky foretold a glorious day.

Before the courteous reader of these pages, the Daimio of Satsuma, hereditary lord over a hundred thousand souls, prostrates himself.

The most noble Lieutenant Sidney Harris, his subordinate, the brave and light-hearted Ensign Walter Budd, and their most faithful and true servant, Ned, have been pleased to appoint me the chronicler of their adventures. I have tried, most illustrious gentlemen, to give a faithful account of our amorous experiences, and in the task of translating the descriptions into potent English, my head and my heart bow down in homage, and worship the helpful genius of the most learned Ensign Budd, whose devotion has repaid me a thousand times for my humble services in guiding both himself and his equally illustrious superior through the joyful and tender mysteries of love. He has often exclaimed, 'There are none who understand the soft arts of amorous experience so well as the Japanese.'

Oh! Beloved kingdom! Source of the Sun! Resplendent in the galaxy of nations! Who can compare to you in the delights of love! Your women are living healthy beams of light, true children of lovely Ten-sio-dai-zin, the Sun Goddess of my native land.

I
THE PARADISE OF LOVE

Know you not, reader, that once the last and greatest of the celestial gods, Iza-na-gi-mikoto spoke to his consort Iza-ni-mi-mikoto thus:

'There should be somewhere a habitable earth. Let us seek it under the waters that are boiling beneath us.'

Thereupon he dipped his jewelled spear into the water with such force that the very firmament rocked and the sun was set burning in the heavens where it now courses. As he withdrew his weapon from the water, the turbid drops that trickled from its end, glistening in the new born light with all the colours of the rainbow, condensed and formed an island. That island was Japan.

'We will dwell there forever! We will call it the Paradise of Love!' cried the innumerable gods, gazing on its resplendent beauties, and the vows they registered a thousand cycles since have yet to be broken.

I am your most humble servant, O dwellers beyond the Seas! I will recount you thrilling scenes of amorous love that will make the warm blood of life leap through your veins. Desire will fill your thoughts to the exclusion of all else. I will permit you to partake with me the most ecstatic pleasure. I will make you sick with love.

I am called Hoyo Ishitura Nanhomu, Daimio of Satsuma, and hereditary lord over a hundred thousand souls. My title is one of honour merely. It no longer has the power that went with it in the days of my ancestors. The noblest blood in all Japan runs through my veins. My father's father was a Royal Prince. Great at one time was our power. Alas for his line! His estates were confiscated, and of a princely domain once a hundred thousand acres, scarcely one thousand remains to me.

Four days after the glorious experiences related in the diary of my good friend Ensign Budd, I had the happy fortune to encounter him again, in company with the honourable Lieutenant Harris and their outspoken underling termed Ned. Most cordial were the greetings that we exchanged with one another.

I was informed that the Lieutenant had been sent on special service for his government, and that he had chosen the others to accompany him. Much was expected of them. Certain astronomical observations of much import to their honourable government were to be made. Six months' leave of absence had been granted in order that they might complete their mission.

'We will make it six months of pleasure in the place of labour,' I told them. 'Listen. The work you are about to engage in has been already performed, and completed, too, in the most perfect manner. Know that a corps of astronomers under my direction have made all the observations and calculations that are necessary. I alone have control of the papers. Exact copies shall be made, and given to you. No one will be the wiser. For six months I will appoint myself your mentor. Follow me, and the gates of paradise will be flung wide open that you may enter and enjoy. I will prove to you that Miyuko is crowded with the most beautiful women to be found in the world. I will introduce to you he whom we term Croesus – the richest merchant in Japan,

The Paradise of Love

Itsogoyu. He will give you a banquet made up of the choicest viands that the earth produces. For dessert you shall have the ripening cunts whose sweetness exceedeth the boasted scents of Araby. Other scenes will be open to you. All the so-called vices that the Japanese are addicted to shall be made known to you. Now what say you?'

'Count upon me!' cried Lieutenant Harris in eager tones.

'And me likewise!' said Ensign Budd.

'I am your servant, masters,' said old Ned.

'*Dai Jobu* – all right!' was my response.

For two weeks did we reside in my Inkyo, or country house. We were in training for the coming joys. We filled our stomachs with selected food. We played like children in the open air. Our days were given up to exercise, and our nights to quiet slumber. Every one of us lived in anticipation of future joys. When the allotted time had elapsed, we were eager to engage in the war of love.

'This coming evening,' I told them, 'we will enjoy the beginning of the feast. Three young and charming Geishas have been engaged to entertain us.'

The old salt, Ned, waxed indignant at my words.

'I beg your honour's pardon, but – look at me prick!'

With these words the servant displayed a member whose hardness appeared to be of iron.

'What, masters, am I to do with this?'

'Soft! Soft!' I interposed. 'Be not too hasty. You are by no means forgotten. Accompanying the Geishas will be a duenna, well practised in the art of taking things like that stiff tool of yours down to nothing. Have no further fears. You are well provided for. Listen. The Geishas are let out by the evening to tea-houses or private parties. From early youth they are trained not only in the art of dancing, but also in the art of what you term fucking. A popular Geisha commands a good price. She has her time overcrowded with engagements. They are witty, quick at repartee, and besides, they would tempt the most holy saint that ever fasted. They are no novices. They are all well broken in. By Izu! They fuck like the mares in heat. Laugh not when I tell you that at times men of high rank take them for wives.'

'Most noble Daimio,' pleaded Lieutenant Harris. 'We tire of lectures. We are nearly wild with desire. Give us action.'

'Yes! Give us action!' cried the others in unison. 'When do they come!'

'Tonight, at the Hour of the Cock (8 p.m.)' was my reply.

'A most appropriately named hour,' commented Ensign Budd.

My palace was situated far from prying eyes. We could pursue our pleasures undisturbed. The Inkyo is privacy itself. Here the Geishas were promptly introduced.

These were the words I spoke:

'I present honourable Americans, Shikibu, the charming Queen of Love, to secure whom it is necessary to engage a year in advance. Next to the black-eyed Isero, the admired one of Tokio, – a score of swains fight constantly for her favours –

'And here I introduce my lovely Seisha, the pride of Satsuma, whom I ardently long to embrace. I have reserved her in advance for myself.

'Last but not least is the stately Murasuka, whose stateliness will be naught when the prick of old Ned stirs her to the screaming point.'

Lieutenant Harris sprang eagerly to the side of Shikibu, and paid her the most delicate attentions in words translated into our Japanese tongue by myself.

'Sweet one!' he cried. 'I kiss your hand. How fortunate am I to be entrusted with such a treasure!'

THE PARADISE OF LOVE

The hot and voluptuous girl gazed at her partner, her eyes swimming with desire.

'You flatter, sir,' she replied.

Then her long black lashes shaded the lovely eyes. The crimson on her cheeks deepened. The ripe red lips opened and disclosed a pearly treasure within.

The Ensign Budd was entranced with the choice I made for him.

'Beautiful Isero!' he exclaimed. 'I am a lucky dog indeed!'

And then old Ned chimed in.

'This Mure – what-you-call'ems – is a nice tidbid. You say she screeches when she fucks? Be Jaysus! Tell her I will make her fat ass crack shell-barks before I am through with her, you bet!'

His figure of speech puzzled me.

'Ass crack shell-barks!' I repeated. 'Pray tell me what the meaning is. We have no equivalent for it in our language. Tell me, so that I can translate it to her. See, she is fairly waiting on our words.'

'A good stiff cock will translate it, then,' returned the strange-speaking old Ned.

The three Geishas now retired for a few moments. Upon their return, they had donned their kimonos (long gowns with wide sleeves, and open in front).

'Oh! What lovely girls!' sighed both Lieutenant Harris and Ensign Budd.

The three stood in front of us and began the dance. From early youth the Geishas are taught to dance. They are charming, graceful and lecherous dancers. You would not hesitate a moment to pronounce them to be such.

Now they swayed their bodies. The kimonos fell open and disclosed their full round bosoms. The artistic management of the draperies was superb. In a trice they changed their gowns, giving us a single instant glance at their lovely posteriors.

'What arses!' I shouted.

'Yes! Yes!' eagerly cried the others. 'They are splendid!'

Now attired in scarlet and yellow, these dainty bits of womanhood imitated with supple bodies, the dance of the maple leaves. One raised her leg high in the air. Oh! What a sight! The rounded calf, swelling thighs, and red-lipped, hairless slit were all shown to us for a second. The entrancing sight made every cock stand erect – a stiffened column of flesh hard as ivory, but tremulous with desire.

It was my charming Seisha who thus displayed her treasures so freely.

Shikibu next came forward. With a swift motion, she threw her kimono over her head. Her naked back, her rounded arse, her well-developed legs and exquisitely moulded calves were exposed to our ardent gaze.

'Oh! It's too beautiful!' cried Lieutenant Harris. 'Oh! It's just magnificent. Oh! If I were only on her now!'

'Oh! My! – Oh! My!' sighed the old Ned. 'What will I do with my cock?'

With this he jumped forward, threw off his breeches and proceeded to dance a sailor's hornpipe with nothing on but his shirt. His ponderous machine stood out like a rod.

We had no time for him, however, for Shikibu turned as if on a pivot and gave us a front view.

'Oh! What breasts!' cried Ensign Budd.

'Just look at the dear cunning little slit!' exclaimed the Lieutenant Harris.

As for your humble servant, I lost command of myself. When the dainty Isero threw herself on the cushion, naked to her neck, and proceeded to work her arse with swiftest motion, the Lieutenant Harris tells me that I stripped myself to the skin, and shouted and danced like a mad person.

'Look at his honour's tool!' shouted old Ned. 'Gee, but ain't it a whopper!'

Even the prim Murasuka herself was affected by the scene. Quickly she threw off her kimono and showed us all her shapely nakedness. She darted forward and seized the old Ned by his tool, and joined him in his dance, closely mimicking every step that he made. Next the Lieutenant Harris, and the Ensign Budd became as naked as myself.

What a lovely sight now presented itself. The three beautiful Geishas had their gowns over their heads, and danced wildly around the apartment.

I chased my darling Seisha. Securing her with a firm grasp I lifted her up in my arms. I bestowed unnumbered kisses on her dainty, pouting slit. Her head hung on my arm. Her rosy tongue worked rapidly in anticipation of the delightful fucking that I was about to give her.

In the meanwhile the Lieutenant Harris had imprisoned his charmer in a corner, and was vigorously working his finger in Shikibu's 'haunt of delight'.

See! She wildly grasps his stiff tool, and fairly screams with joy as she writhes, twists and plunges under his skillful touchings.

The Ensign Budd, I notice, has placed his head between Isero's thighs, and seems never to tire of kissing and fondling the gate of her paradise.

How different is the old Ned! He is on top of Murasuka, crying.

'By God! This is the tightest hole I ever struck! Something's got to bust before I git in! – Bah! I'm off! – It's easy now. – Work your ass, Mary! – Work like hell! – How do you like my liver-toucher? Oh! Oh! – This is good enough for the Admiral. – Oh! You are a fucker from 'way-back.'

As for me, I place my Seisha with her arse on the pillow. Her red-lined slit is a prominent mark. I tease her with the head of my prick. I rub her clitoris with the head of my tool.

'Ah! This a hanami (picnic) well worth going to,' I cry, as my prick stretches her slit open.

As I push my way onward, the Geisha bites my shoulder. When my prick is in her, when my hair reaches the lips of her little haven of pleasure, I clasp my hands around her arse – this is my favourite style – and press her closer still.

'Ah! This is heaven!' I cry.

As I dance around, with my impaled partner, her legs close tightly around me, clasping me as in a vice. I bump her plump backside against the back of the Lieutenant Harris, who is working his arse like an engine. The weight of our bodies causes him to halt. Gentle heaves now succeed the swifter ones.

I fuck my partner on top of the Lieutenant's arse. In a moment or so he regains his breath, and with it apparently new energy. He recommences action, timing his motions with mine. The combined action in unison – the two couples fucking as one – adds much to our bliss, and makes our partners fairly scream with delight. Then we pause, and look about us.

The Ensign Budd is still in the corner, slapping his partner's arse. The slaps are at times so loud as to echo throughout the apartment. At the same time, he is working his prick (it's quite a strong member, by the way) in and out of the dainty little Isero's slit. You could see her fairly sucking it in. For, as he withdraws, you may observe the inner foldings of her pleasure-font displaying themselves.

As he enters her entirely, they totally disappear.

'Oh! Lord! Where did you learn to fuck so fine!' cries the enraptured Ensign Budd.

As he speaks thus, he begins to fuck her with wonderful swiftness. His strokes come so thick and fast, that my eyes, used as they are to such sights, can scarcely follow, much less keep count of them.

'Oh! What a sight!' I cry, loudly.

Then I commenced to work my own arse again. Every shove I gave her increased my ecstasy. We fell off the Lieutenant, leaving him to his own devices. My partner's shapely legs relaxed, and she lay beneath me, panting and almost motionless. I twined my heavy limbs about my partner's plump back, and shot my hot stream of lava into her very vitals. Then I removed her mouth from my shoulders. I placed it to my own. I sucked it closely, insinuated my tongue, and worked it just as the old Ned said he did. I thrilled with joy, pricking me all over like needles. Then in my agony of delight, I shot another stream of semen into the quivering girl under me, that made her moan with joy.

'Hurrah!' shouted the old Ned. 'I have got another hard-on!'

'You waste your words,' I said. 'Your partner knows not the meaning of the term, "hard-on".'

'I will let her feel it – then she'll know the meaning!' he loudly responded. 'There, girlee! Take that! – My! My! But she wobbles! Whoa! Girlee! Keep your ass still till I stick it in! – Now, git up, girlee! Git up! Wobble your ass! Wobble! Wobble! – That's the style! – Oh! That's good! That's fine! That takes the biscuit! – Look out for me, girlee! – I am going to squirt! There I go again! – Whoop! Whoop! – Bah! I am a dead busted rooster!'

She squirmed and twisted with amorous satisfaction as

he rolled off her, and lay there, quivering and panting. The old salt, Ned, had given her a realization of some of her daydreams.

We were all halted now. Nature was for a time satisfied.

'To the pool!' I cry, a short time after the agony of delight has expired.

Speaking thus, I lead the way to the bathing saloon. This is a long room, containing a pool of water twenty feet long by ten feet wide. A glass-covered roof is over the apartment. Innumerable lanterns make this place as bright as day.

In a trice, eight naked forms are immersed in the tepid water. The Japanese, I would have you understand, are the greatest bathers in the world. They are forever bathing. For that reason, they are the healthiest among nations.

Soon the Geishas are as sportive as naiads. One moment they are floating on their backs, displaying their pouting slits, which look as fresh as if they belonged to virgins. Not the slightest evidence of their ever having been parted by stiffened pricks could be noticed. I had thought that my goodly tool would have made its mark upon Seisha's portals of heavenly bliss, but they look as fresh and tempting as those of a maiden.

But not so, however, with Murasuka. The duenna's slit was slightly open, as though it were gasping for air, and displayed the red ripe lining within. The old Ned had trounced it well with his mighty tool.

What sport it was for us! How the merry, laughing sprites fled from one end of the pool to the other! They swam and dived like so many ducks. One moment the hand would grasp a plump thigh. The next second it had slipped away.

The old Ned puffed and blowed like a big porpoise.

'These here cunt-pieces is as slippery as eels,' he commented.

[You will notice, kind reader, that I give the old Ned's language as he spoke it. Many of his words are unfamiliar to me. Search as I will in the dictionary of your language, I cannot find them defined.]

The Lieutenant Harris and the Ensign Budd were excellent swimmers. The Geishas, however were their superiors.

'I would like to try one of them spring chicken ones!' cried the old Ned, attempting to seize a fairy-like form as she passed.

The Geishas laughingly shook their heads in derision if not denial.

'It seems, Ned,' shouted out the Ensign Budd, 'as though you were never satisfied with your partner. Murasuka will be jealous.'

'Oh! She's fine! – I was only a fooling,' returned the old salt.

When tired of our water-sport, we repaired to a table crowded with delicacies such as we of the Japanese nobility alone know how to purchase. Champagne took the place of saki, and our spirits became greatly heightened by the nectar, that we drank. We sat naked at the feast, and at its conclusion gave away to the sexual desires within us.

The sweet little angel Isero placed both of her rosy little feet on the table. After the remains of the feast were removed, she sprang upon the table, and filled us with inexpressible delight by dancing in the most lascivious manner.

The other two joined her, and meanwhile we lolled amorously backward to enjoy the enchanting scene.

Seisha and Isero now ardently embrace one another. They place their fingers in one another's slits and dance around, working vigorously as they go. This evidently causes them the most exquisite sensations. Their eyes are turned upwards in ecstatic pleasure. Then their arses work furiously. Quicker and quicker go their fingers. Now they move their bottoms slowly but vigorously. You can see their bellies slap together. Next, they glue themselves to each other. The spendings are seen to trickle slowly down their legs.

'Now is the time, boy!' I shouted. 'They would take anything that would fuck. They are hot with desire! They are wild with lechery. They want to be fucked bad. The harder you give it to them, the better they like it.'

I had no need to say more. The Lieutenant Harris lifted the delighted Isero from the table and placed her on a cushion. He could not be quick enough, for she seized his tool and kissed it ravenously. Then he sucked at her lips as though he could feast on them forever. Next she placed his stiffened prick in her devouring slit, worked him between her thighs and fucks his mouth with her tongue.

'By God! That must be fine!' shouted the old Ned.

' 'Tis the Ensign's turn!' I cried. 'We four will look. Our turn will soon arrive.'

The Ensign Budd whirls his partner around the room – kissing, sucking – now down on the floor with arses moving rapidly. Then up they jump, and waltz around – his fine prick wholly encased in the tight little slit.

Now he reaches the table.

'A cushion!' he cries.

One is thrown to him. He removed his penis, which is still as stiff as ever. He places his partner face downward, her ripe bosom resting on the cushion. Then he raises her legs between his arms and thrusts his prick straight in the splendid mark. Then he withdraws it a bit, just enough to let him bend his face downward to her arse and kiss it. He playfully bites it, and then thrusts in to the very full, remaining almost motionless in keen enjoyment.

'Ha! Most noble Daimio!' he shouts, 'I cannot spend, yet every second I think I am going to. By Christ! This is better than Heaven! Oh! She grips me like a vice.'

The old Ned, who was playing furiously with his partner's slit, cries out at this juncture.

'Look at the lucky dog! He's got into a slut and is hitched fast! Throw a bucket of water over them!'

By Iza! I believe the old rascal was right, for the Ensign Budd could not release himself, try as he would. He only plunged deeper into her, and bit at her shoulder till she winced. The marks of his teeth showed livid on her olive skin.

The Lieutenant Harris was still engaged with his partner. Gentle heaves on the part of both told the story of extreme pleasure. The previous encounter had temporarily exhausted the seminal fluid, thus permitting them to enjoy to the full the greatest of all delights.

The Ensign Budd lifted his partner from the table, and was sprawling on her among the cushions on the floor. At intervals he would roll over so that she was on top of him. He would raise her to the very top of his prick, then press her arse till the lips of her slit were buried in his hair.

We four lookers-on were now wrought up to the very highest pitch by the entrancing performance of the others.

I long to enjoy the charms of Shikibu. I place her on the cushions. I begin to work my prick into her clinging slit.

'Oh! How thick!' she cries in Japanese. 'Oh! Lovely prick! I feel you all over. The other was long! This is thick. Oh! Master, fuck me hard! I want it! I am dying for it! Give me your tongue! I will lick your lips! Permit me, sweet Lord, to kiss your thick tool!'

I take it out of her tight slit. She greedily kisses it, and then mouths it as though it were some dainty morsel that she is about to swallow. But sucking is something I will not permit. I withdraw it, and replace it in the proper orifice. I push it with vigorous thrusts, to which she responds by working her arse from one side to the other, causing us both the most exquisite pleasure.

'Dear Lord,' she whispers, 'just let us be still a few moments. Then carry me around the room, and push my arse against the wall. – Dear, dear Lord! I want to kiss your thick thing. Oh! It feels so splendid! – There! Fuck my tongue – I will suck your lips! – Dear, dear Lord! I come again! Don't you feel it all over your thing? Now let us both work our arses together.'

And work I did, too. I gave it to her with rapid thrusts. One moment I would pull out my prick and place it near her mouth. She would kiss it greedily. Then back it would go into the reddened slit.

The Japanese do not as a rule indulge in the beastly acts of the so-called civilized nations. What is termed by you buggering, or penetration of the anus, is seldom practised. Neither is abuse of the divine sexual organs by sucking. Occasionally some degraded Japanese who has learned the bestial depths of forbidden pleasure in foreign climates, or perhaps some Chinese prostitute, will do so, but for my part it is disgusting to me. Had I the power, I would decree that the perpetrators of such bestiality should instantly suffer the death penalty. We may indulge in voluptuous enjoyment to the full, but when it descends to foul bestiality, we halt instantly.

Kissings and fondlings of the sexual organs are naturally practised by the Japanese, as they are by the most savage nations that exist on the face of the earth.

But to resume.

When I felt that the final crisis was not far away, I carried my lovely Shikibu around the pool. My prick was tightly encased in her salacious slit.

Oh! How can I find words to describe the state of my feelings? I would push the plump arse against the wall, then run forward a few yards. Next I would halt, and slap the cheeks of the posteriors with vigorous blows. In my mad flight, I saw no obstruction until I fell helter-skelter over the old Ned, who was giving the finishing touches to his final screw.

'Where in hell are you going?' he shouts, in his rough way.

We are on top of them with our arses moving at rapid rate. In smothered tones he cries out to me:

'Whoa! Whoa! Get off! – You'll break my cock off! – Get off, I tell you!'

I rolled off and now, being in a good position, I gave my partner a good load of semen. Not satisfied with this, I held on. I convulsively moved my arse, and gave her another good squirt.

This was my final effort. My tool fell out, and the overjoyed girl rolled on the floor – her feet rising up and down rapidly. Next her arse, trembling with pleasure, moved quickly from side to side. Then up would come the sweet little slit as if eagerly seeking a new prick to gratify its greedy mouth.

This fine sight exercised an instant magnetic influence. My prick became hardened in a single second to the rigidity of iron. Like a vulture I descended upon the red-lined beauty before me. I kissed it greedily for a few minutes. Then I placed the head of my tool between the cunning lips.

I hear her whisper sweet nothings. She has lost command of herself.

'Dear Lord! Your thing tickles me! Oh! it tickles me so

STATES OF ECSTASY

splendid! Oh! It's just too heavenly! – Just let us be still a while. I feel your dear thing way in me! – Now work, and I will work too! – Dear Lord! Push away! – Now give it me! Hard as you can! – We will both work together! – That's the way!' she fondly shrieks.

'I am not done! I will not squirt more for a while. By Smika! I will hold this back! I want to keep this up forever!' Then I shouted loudly, 'Everybody fuck! Fuck like men that haven't had a woman for a year!'

'See here, old boy,' the old Ned answered. 'I can't fuck any harder. This here cunt-piece has nearly broke me back! She'll have me fucked out soon. Then I'll have to quit. – Hold your horses, Daisy! – Hold your horses! – Ouch! – Me God! I've squirted!'

Now I begin to push. The path of pleasure is yielded inch by inch. Then I work my arse fiercely. When my prick is in her to the full, when my bag of cream slaps against her gates of pleasure, something within her seems to twine itself about the head of my badge of manhood. I thrust – thrust – Oh! What exquisite delight! I insert my tongue between her willing lips, and drop into a rapturous slumber, dreaming of paradise.

How long I remained thus I know not. Suddenly, without the slightest motion I felt myself coming. I squirted a continuous stream into her. This was truly my last effort.

'See! The Daimio's pumped out at last!' I heard Lieutenant Harris say. His voice came to me like a voice in a dream. 'Come, boys, let's go to bed.'

And the old Ned added:

'Oh! What a sick-looking cock I've got. Just look at him, masters! He's been on a drunk and is all broke up! – Good Lord! But can't these Japs fuck?'

II
THE JUGGLER AND THE NUNS

After the amorous combat which I have just related, we all slept long and peacefully. Nature was tired out. Such unusuals calls as we had made upon her caused us to seek recuperation in much-needed repose.

The sun was just setting when we were once more assembled at the banquet table. The Geishas had returned to their respective abodes.

'We are through with that crowd,' the old Ned sententiously expressed it. 'Now trot out your other fuckers!'

'Soft!' I replied. 'Be not so greedy. We will not stir from this place for a fortnight. Meanwhile we will be wise, and renew our fallen energies. For the next adventure may prove more enervating than the last.'

'Respected sir,' returned the Lieutenant Harris, 'we all thank you for the most pleasant entertainment which your kindness provided for us.'

'Let me add,' observed the Ensign Budd, 'that I never enjoyed myself so much before.'

'Oh! It was the finest cunt-piece I ever struck!' chimes in the old Ned. 'Oh! How sore my balls are! I think that Mare – Mary – whatever her name is, has pumped me dry.'

'I am greatly pleased, most noble Americans,' I replied,

'at your expressions of gratification. Think not, however, that the few days of deprivation will tire you. I have secured the services of the most entertaining narrator in all Japan. This man, Jatsakura by name, is a professional storyteller, whose services are by no means easy to secure. By solemn contract with the Mikado, every good story must first be told to the monarch. Jatsakura must discover or invent some new feature to cater to the voluptuousness of our Emperor; and what is more, it must have truth for its foundation. The story that you will hear to-night comes fresh from the Mikado's palace.

'We will spend our days as previously in the open air. We will enjoy the most succulent food. Let us take care to thoroughly exercise our bodies. Should we find that our bodies are sufficiently recuperated, we will shorten the allotted time.'

'Oh! It won't take me long to get a hard-on,' said the old Ned.

'Ha! Ha!' laughed the Lieutenant Harris, 'But can you keep it? As we are now, one little squirt could we give, and we are done.'

The following evening Jatsakura made his appearance. The tale that he related is as follows:

Masters, I bow myself humbly before your august presences. I crave the pleasure of having your honourable ears for a little while, and perhaps what I am about to say may possess a little grain of merit that may please your omnipotent sensibilities. I crave your indulgence then for the story of The Juggler and the Nuns.

You know – if not, permit me to tell you – that Yase is a village near Kyoto or Mikao. It is situated at the base of Hizer-Zan, the historic Buddhist stronghold. In this place the men, but more especially the women, attain a stature and muscular development quite unique. They are all strong, jolly, red-cheeked. They are as amorous as fettlesome mares in heat.

I need not tell you that they understand the mysteries of love better than all else in Japan. That they are the most enjoyable creatures to be met, and that they can prolong the sexual agony in the most delightful and enticing manner. Their fame has travelled over the great earth. They have among them visitors from all climes, whose lechery is such that their own people cannot satisfy them. Let me tell you here that no stranger is admitted to practise the rites of Venus at Yase without the most rigid and searching medical examination.

'Be God!' interjected the old Ned. 'No feller with the pox can get in there!'

Jatsakura looked severely at the old sailor.

'I am not accustomed to interruption,' he querulously observed. 'Let it not occur again.'

The Lieutenant Harris seriously reprimanded his underling.

The art of cohabitation (continued the narrator) is taught from early youth. As soon as the child arrives at the proper age, he or she is taught the mysteries of love. The teacher's position is a most delightful and pleasant occupation, for it is his duty to take the maiden-heads of all the young virgins. Ages of practice have made them perfect. They cohabit as regularly as they eat.

Many of the women are nuns in the Buddhist monastery on the top of the mountain. In this convent, what you term chastity is not ranked with the other virtues. It is believed by them that the divine Buddha invented the sexual organs for the purpose of strengthening his religious tenets. His sacred words have come down to us. They are as follows:

'Mortals, I give to you the power to prolong your lives for unnumbered generations. With this power I will add unlimited joy, so that the male will seek the female, and in the delicious agonies of blissful ecstasy implant into her fruitful womb the seed that will reproduce themselves.'

Not all the beauties of the town were to be found, however, in its precincts. Numbers at an early age entered the convent on the top of the mountain, where I can assure you that not all of their time was given up to the practice of religion. The worship of the sexual organs is a most prominent feature in connection with more sacred things. Amida's – Buddha's – teachings embrace many things relating to sexuality.

Now there lived in Kyoto a juggler, Hai-Ka by name. He was celebrated for his skill, throughout all Japan. He was a man of great strength and beauty of person. Likewise was he famous as the possessor of an enormous prick. Its strength and size were proverbial. The ballad writers had composed numerous songs about it, and our epic poet O-Kari-San wrote a thousand verses in its praise. The fame of its stiffness had travelled to Mikao, and by some means which I am not able to explain to you, had come to the ears of the favourite wife of the Mikado, who was said to be the most beautiful woman in the world – Zai-ka-mata.

Rumour saith that the Emperor was the possessor of so many wives as to be scarcely able to satisfy one. Naturally, the imprisoned women were great sufferers. Generous living increased their desires; and it is said that they held weekly unions and gratified themselves by fucking one another for hours with their fingers or bamboo skibi-sticks.

The Juggler and the Nuns

Now Zai, tiring of a wooden prick, sighed for one of flesh and blood. She therefore determined to travel in disguise, enter the convent, bribe the nuns, and enjoy the good things that Hai-Ka's prick would alone bestow.

Hai-Ka was in great demand, not only for his skill as a juggler, but also for the wide reputation he possessed as the owner of the finest implement of masculine persuasion in all Japan.

Even the little girls of the town had heard of this tool. Sometimes they followed him about as ewes do the ram, beseeching him, coaxing him, begging him to show them his treasure.

Rumour has it that one day a number of girls, just released from school, met him on the corner of a retired street.

'Ha! Good Hai-Ka,' shouted a pert miss of sixteen. 'We have you now! Come! Give us a sight of that of which we have heard so much!'

In order to induce him to assent, the little angel threw her attire above her head, and gave Hai-ka a sight of the sweetest little slit that his eyes had ever beheld. What prick could withstand such a temptation? Certainly not Hai-Ka's, for his tool rose to such a ponderous size and stiffness that it burst its bonds, and stood out like a crane. A shout of admiration arose from the lips of the amorous girls. One sprang forward and fondled its purple head. Some walked beneath it, and gazed in awe-struck admiration. One little thing placed her two hands upon it and raised herself from the ground with its aid.

With one voice they cry:

'How is it possible that our little slits could ever contain such a monster?'

To which Hai-Ka responds:

'Out of the smallest slits come the biggest babies.'

With these words he covered his tool and hastened away.

Hai-Ka served the nuns in the convent at stated intervals. On these occasions bacchanalian orgies would usurp the worship of Buddha. It was at the beginning of one of these festivals that the Empress Zai-ka-mata arrrived secretly to witness the ceremonies with the hope of participating in them.

The first act that Hai-Ka was to perform began just as the greatest lady in the land entered. The apartment contained a score of women and six men – the latter being all splendid specimens of manhood. The juggler was entirely naked. He was seated in the centre of the apartment. Reposing upon a rich cushion in front of him was a beaufitul girl of sixteen. She, too, was in a nude state.

Hai-Ka was gradually exciting himself. One moment his hands were on her breasts. Next they were softly pressing the delicate lips of her slit. His prick was a sight to behold. Slowly it rose to its majestic length. Truly rumour had not falsely stated its proportions. It was enormous.

Meanwhile he has placed the girl's thighs across his loins, bringing her 'love-mouth' close to his own.

Then he begins to address it in a sing-song tone:

'Pretty red lips! Dear little ruby slit! See it stick out! Isn't it a treasure? See! I touch it. Now she moves her arse up and down – up and down! – That's a sweet girl – Isn't that delicious? See! I rub the precious little thing that makes her arse move quicker. – That's a dear one! Rub my prick! – See these tight folds! Nature cries aloud! She wants the prick of man? – Oh! So badly! – Oh! She wants it all! – Yes, I will soon part those precious lips. – See! I kiss and kiss them! See! I work my finger thus. Watch her move her arse again. – Isn't it sublime? – We all ought to worship this. It is the feast of all feasts! Now she spends! She spends – No prick has entered here! And soon she will scream with bliss! – Oh! Ho! The way is oiled. – For behold, she spends again!'

After a pause he resumes again:

'Now watch me work my prick! There! It is going in! – Ah! Siako! But it is good! I give an extra strong push! Harken! Just hear her shriek! She has lost her maidenhead! – And now my way is clear! Up! Up! I go. – Oh! watch her eager anxious lips! They are dying to be kissed! – I suck – and suck – and suck! – I fuck – and fuck – and fuck! – Great Buddha! Hear my thanks! Was ever bliss like this? – Ah! I cannot hold it back! – Now see! She rolls her eyes! Her shrieks are loud and long! Now I am in her to the full! – Oh! Lovely one! Be still! – Let us repose a while!'

For a moment silence reigns. Then he begins once more.

'Now kiss! And kiss! And kiss again! – Again! A sweeter kiss! – My arse must move again! I cannot keep it still! – Take that! And that! And that! – Oh! By Iza! Let me stay! – By the gods! I cannot hold it back! – I am off! And off again! No longer can I halt it! The stream of life is coming in its richest flow! – Behold the blissful moment! – Gautama! How I thank you! – The organ now has spent! Disturb her not. Oh! Sisters! Leave us to ourselves for a few minutes. Ah! – Her joy is beyond expression!'

During this exciting scene the nuns were greatly affected. They laughed. They sang. They danced. The Empress joined them in the orgy.

'I come,' she cries, 'from the palace of the Mikado! Your lives will pay the forfeit should you betray me.'

With these words, the fairest of the fair threw off her

apparel, and in a frenzy of sexual passion danced round and round the apartment. The nuns quickly followed her example. Likewise did the strong-limbed men of Yase.

Meanwhile Hai-Ka and the newly-made woman were wrapped in each other's arms.

'I am come to enjoy the famous prick of Hai-Ka!' shrieked the lustful Empress.

As she spoke thus, all eyes were fastened upon this matchless specimen of womanhood. Her limbs were round and plump. Her bosoms two priceless hemispheres. Her face was the personification of beauty. The olive-tinged cheeks were flushed with crimson beauty. Her eyes outshone the brilliance of the diamonds around her neck. Her sweet mouth was a perfect Cupid's bow, displaying in its small opening pearl outvying the most priceless gems of ocean's treasures. Her long black hair was loose, and all but covered the rounded cheeks of her dimpled arse. But when she danced and discovered to us a view of her sweetest of charms – her lovely slit – the expressions that arose were loud and ardent. The lips pouted in the most entrancing manner. They showed themselves more prominent than is usual with a woman. A line of reddened beauty marked their limits.

The men halted to worship. One lusty fellow, with a splendidly proportioned prick, bowed his head before her.

'There is a woman awaiting you! – I have come for Hai-Ka,' she sternly said, pointing to a very Venus, whose blushing countenance showed the strong desire within her.

For an answer, the excited man turns to the waiting Venus to whom he has been directed. He seizes her as a tiger does his prey. He kisses her exposed beauties times without number. He then pushes his glorious prick into her waiting slit and they both proceed to battle sexually with each other in the fiercest manner.

THE JUGGLER AND THE NUNS

The rest of the women become likewise excited. They strive with one another to obtain a man. Having obtained him, they lock him in their arms, twine their thighs across his back, and sigh and shriek with joy.

Meanwhile Hai-Ka has released himself from the arms of his late partner, and turns to the goddess who is awaiting him.

'Mighty Mistress!' he cries, bowing his head until he touches the floor. 'What fortune is before me! In the light of your favour I am doubly blessed!'

'Rise, Hai-Ka,' commands the eager Empress. 'I would see this mighty instrument of thine.'

The recumbent one arose. At the sight of her glorious slit, his prick stiffened to proportions wonderful to behold.

The Empress becomes wild with joy.

' 'Tis nought but truth! Hai-Ka, I did not dream of such a noble instrument as this. They were right. You are the owner of the greatest prick in all Japan.'

'And you,' responds the juggler, 'art the possessor of the most lovely cunt in all the wide domain of Japan.'

'Meet then is it,' she observes, 'that we should come together for an hour: for you art now the Emperor, the king of kings of all Japan and the adjacent islands and I, I am your humble mistress.'

The enraptured juggler is now thoroughly intoxicated with joy. Fortune had indeed blessed him. What! He, an humble juggler, in possession of the most beautiful woman in all Japan?

'Am I dreaming?' quoth he.

Warm kisses soon convinced him that he was not.

At the sight of his magnificent penis, the Empress had become a slave. She falls upon her knees before him. Oh! How she fondles his prick! With what delight she weighs his heavy balls. She waters its head with her dainty tongue. She kisses it from end to end.

'What raptures will be mine!' she cries. 'By all the gods! I could not lose this for a paradise! Soon it will pierce me to the full! Yes, I know I will shriek, and sob, and cry with joy. How delightful is the anticipation! Why, my Hai-Ka, the Mikado's prick is all but useless. A fuck from him only creates further desire, for hardly does he enter than he spends. Oh! How many, many times have I longed for a good tool that would pierce me to the quick! And now – thanks to Amida! – I am to be gratified!'

'Sublime majesty,' returns Hai-Ka, 'I shall do my best to please you.'

Saying this, he falls upon his knees and repeatedly kisses the red-ripe lips of her glowing slit. After each kiss, she gently moves her arse. For now her whole body is quivering with blissful anticipation.

The rest of the company have now ceased their amorous play. The tender scenes that were now about to be enacted possessed sufficient attraction to enchain their closest attention.

The juggler's prick was truly a grand sight. The women's eyes were all rivetted upon its noble proportions.

'Companions – for such I now call you,' said the Empress, 'in the presence of such a tool as this we are all equals. Modesty and pride of station fall prostrate before this.'

Speaking thus, she caught hold of Hai-Ka's penis, and led him around by it, going to each woman in turn. They gaze upon it with eager straining eyes, for most of them had enjoyed its ripeness, and knew its power to please.

The nuns sat on the cushions, with a man between them. One possessed the fallen prick, the other laid claim to the

THE JUGGLER AND THE NUNS

balls. On their part, the men buried their hands in the magnificent slits on both sides of them, and toyed and teased the ardent women around them.

The Empress reclined on the cushions, with her arse high in the air. Her magnificent slit jutted out most prominently, displaying its beauties to the fullest advantage. Before it, a shrine, the half-crazed Hai-Ka again knelt in worship.

'Lovely slit!' he cries. 'Delightful crevice! Heavenly grotto! I will soon enter you! I will cause our great mistress to sob and shriek with joy. I will shoot again and again into her innermost recesses the water of life.'

'What a hell of a big cock he must have had!' remarked the old Ned, in a low tone.

The narrator paused in his tale. I ceased its translation. The Lieutenant Harris angrily rebuked his underling. Jatsakura looked from one to the other, and finally his glance settled upon me. As best I could, I explained the meaning of the remark. Jatsakura nodded, smiled broadly at the old Ned, who returned with a grin, a diabolical leer and a knowing wink. Then the tale was resumed.

Hai-Ka continued, winding up his adoration of the Empress's cunt as follows:

'I will open up for his majesty the Emperor a slit that has been closed too long.'

'Yes, now!' cries the eager woman.

Meanwhile the Empress keeps up the gentle to and fro movements of her arse, causing all the other men present to play a little roughly with their partners.

The juggler now commences to play with his eager partner. He teases her clitoris until she works her arse furiously with delight. Finally she gives an extra frantic upheaval.

Then the spendings can be noticed flowing out of her excited crevice. One of the nuns acts as hand-maiden, and softly bathes the exposed parts.

The juggler now kisses the moist slit most greedily. Then he inserts the head of his tool between the oiled lips. It enters easily. Then he commences to work his loins fiercely; while she, enjoying it to the full, remains still. He removes his tool. He places it to her mouth. She kisses and fondles it with her lips, then motions him to replace it. He returns it to the tightened haunt of love, and again moves his arse with astonishing rapidity. Great Iza! How he fucks her! 'Ah! Ah!'s and 'He! He!'s come from her. Little shrieks follow. Her tongue hangs out of her mouth, and works in unison with his tool. She moans. She cries. For the juggler is fucking her as she was never fucked before. Now her belly springs forward to meet his. Resounding slaps are now heard by all.

'Oh! Oh! Oh!' she shouts. 'Move your arse quicker, slave, or I will have your head taken off! – You are slow! – Come, move yourself!'

Saying this, she met his shove with a most vigorous thrust of her belly, and threw him a full yard back flat on the floor. Her limbs twist frantically about. In a second he is back to her devouring slit. Again he enters. Up he goes, until nothing is seen of his tool. Then she digs her heels into his back and holds him in a vice-like embrace.

The on-lookers are much affected by this distracting sight. The women, also excited by the fingering, again fight eagerly for a man. Hardly has a slit received a stiffened prick and had two or three shoves from it than it is removed, and another gaping cunt is pushed forward to secure the coveted treasure.

The now everjoyed Empress breaks the silence. 'I am

The Juggler and the Nuns

gorged with the supremest delicacy that epicures ever invented!' she cries. 'This is a new dish and – Oh! What appetite I have to enjoy it. – No! – I will not lose the juggler. Hizer-Zan, the strong-hold of Buddha, the divine, shall see me whored before its very eyes. Your chadai (gold) shall be enough to enrich you all your days, O Hai-Ka. – Ha! You answer me with a flow of scalding semen! – Amida! Amida! I call upon you. Let Hai-Ka maintain his stiffness!'

The juggler had emptied his treasure bags. He withdrew his tool for a moment.

'By Saika! It is as stiff as ever! Buddha has answered my prayer!'

Now commenced the true battle of love. The preliminary struggle is but an excitant of prolonged pleasure. See! How grandly he fucks her. Observe, too, what a superb return she gives! Her stomach meets his at every thrust! He pulls her down from the cushions. Fastened together by his enormous link of pleasure, they jump a few feet. Again he pushes her down, and fucks with lightning thrusts. He withdraws his mighty prick to its very head, and then forces it back into its greedy receptacle.

Scream upon scream peals from the lips of the Empress. Now she sucks his lips. See! She digs her fingers into his back convulsively. Then she sinks her milk-white teeth into his shoulder until he in turn loudly cries out. She licks his face, his mouth. Again they rise. He grasps the plump cheeks of her arse and jumps with her high in the air, his prick all the while working inside of her by wonderful muscular action. See how he trembles! Nature cannot hold back much longer. He places her arse right between the thighs of one of the most beautiful nuns. She clasps the Empress in close embrace.

Hai-Ka once more moves his arse with astonishing speed. He halts a moment. Then he shoots into the greedy woman a burning stream of molten lava. The Empress with a profound sigh of satisfaction falls back. Hai-Ka rolls off her, falls heavily to the floor, and lies there inert, motionless, like a log, His mighty prick has dwindled down to flabby nothingness.

Zai-ka-ma ta comes to herself. She rises! She throws herself upon Hai-Ka as he lies there prostrate. She places her hand between his thighs, and fondles the dwindled monarch that had administered to her late pleasures. Then rapturously she kisses a thousand times the glorious tool that had made her feel the most exquisite of earthly joys.

Speaking thus, Jatsakura, paused. Then he turned to us.

'Most noble hearers! May the sunshine never be darkened for you. I have finished. I have told you all I am permitted to tell about the Juggler and the Nuns, of which the incident of the coming of Empress Zai is but the first part. Until his imperial Majesty has approved of the remainder of my tale, I cannot offer it to you. I thank you for your kindness in listening. I am your humblest slave, my lord Daimio.'

Up started the old Ned, holding his stiff tool in his hands.

'A cunt! I want a cunt!' he shouts.

'Yes!' cry the Lieutenant Harris and the Ensign Budd. 'We all want cunts!'

The narrator of the story regarded us with a smile half of triumph, half of lechery. His prick I could see stood firm and erect, pressing out his kimono into a little mountain between his thighs. Even his translator was greatly excited.

'I too want a cunt!' I cry aloud. 'Well, we shall have them. A week hence will find us in Kkoto (Mikao). The merchant Itsogoyu is now hunting all Japan for novelties. By Amida the glorious! You shall have cunts that will twist your very stones!'

'I guess I'll have a little jerk all to myself!' says the old Ned.

With this he retires to a corner, where his actions indicate to us that he is not only carrying out his intentions, but deriving a great deal of pleasure from the act, that is, if the expression on his face told the truth.

'Never mind, Petey,' says the old Ned. 'You will feel better soon.'

He is talking to his stiff tool, along which his hand fondly wanders.

'Come, now! Be a good boy! – Spit, you devil! Spit! – Spit, I tell you! – Oh! You won't? Then I'll make you! – Ah! That's real good! That's fine! – Yum! Yum! – Hist! Now we're off!'

III
THE MERCHANT ITSOGOYU

Behold us, attentive reader, once more prepared for the amorous fray. With bodies refreshed by choice foods and healthful exercise, we are again ready to worship at the shrine of love. My good Itsogoyu, who obliges me in all things, did not fail me in this, my latest request. Upon our arrival at his magnificent residence in Mikao (Kyoto, as the foreign ones name it) we were all received with that generous welcome and lavish hospitality for which the merchant prince is famed.

'This mansion and all within it are at your disposal. Welcome, most honorable Lord and worthy Americans, to the house of Itsogoyu.'

These were the words which he spoke. Willing servitors led us to the bath, where all traces of our long travelling were dissipated. We were conducted to perfumed rooms where soft and soothing notes of the kamisan (guitar) lulled our senses into soft slumber.

After our short siesta followed the banquet. Eight courses made up the dinner. Viands fit for the most fastidious epicure were spread before us in lavish profusion. The table was a masterpiece of ivory carved by an artist whose time is worth a fortune, and most skilfully inlaid with massive gold. It alone must have been worth more than all I ever possessed. The bills, legs, and claws of the birds served us were covered with gold leaf.

'Does he eat gold?' asked the Ensign Budd with a merry twinkle in his eye.

The solemn look which accompanied my nod in the affirmative made the old Ned open his eyes and mouth in wonder. It was with the utmost difficulty that I could keep countenance.

The choicest of wines from every quarter of the globe formed a part of each course.

The old Ned moved uneasily in his seat.

'If we are to have cunts for a dessert,' he suddenly shouts, 'why turn 'em out. I feel as ornery as a bull!'

A kick from the Lieutenant Harris restrained further speech. Itsogoyu, looking wonderingly at me, inquired the cause of the outburst. I laughingly evaded his request, but the merchant would not have it so.

'Cunts! Cunts!' he repeats. 'That is what I heard the English say. Is it one of their gods? Do they worship cunts?'

I translated his remarks to my companions. They shout with laughter.

'You bet your boots, old cock!' coarsely observes the old Ned, safe in his host's ignorance of the language. 'Oh! Don't we love cunt, though? Why, we worship it, don't we, masters?'

This sally occasioned renewed laughter.

At the time of which I write, the merchant Itsogoyu was in the prime of manhood. His age was forty-seven. His wealth was estimated at fifty millions of your dollars. Therefore there was nothing on this earth buyable that he could not buy. His palace outwardly was much inferior to the magnificent abode of the Mikados. As a humble citizen, liable to have his fortune forfeited in a single moment, prudence forbade any outward show. In its universal beauty and lavish adornment, it exceeded any palace in the

The Merchant Itsogoyu

whole realm of Japan. Despite the fact that the great wealth of Itsogoyu excited jealousy, he had contrived to increase it daily. At one time he had been called upon by the Daimio of Mikao on behalf of his master, to contribute half a million gold yen. To this demand he instantly complied. He also gave much to charity. No deserving one appealed to him for aid in vain.

Itsogoyu possessed a remarkably handsome face. Many a woman would have fallen deeply in love at the sight of his splendid features. His was a well-knit form, handsome, graceful, and supple. He had muscles of iron endurance beneath a fair, delicate and rather effeminate skin. His many gifts made him a great favourite with the gentler sex.

We were well filled with the bounteous repast. The time now came when our full stomachs craved a rest. Repletion followed. Then while we were resting on our divans, the merchant clapped his hands.

In response to this signal the embroidered curtains were thrust aside and two lovely Geishas entered with graceful step. Their only covering was their long black hair.

They were scarce seventeen years of age, and beautiful beyond description. Their forms were the perfection of beauty. Their ripe bosoms were distracting to behold. Their shapely thighs would have made a sculptor envious. And as for the dainty little slits, oh! How can I find words enough to tell you about them?

'Oh! It'll bust my cock!' cries the old Ned. 'My! But ain't this a fine dessert?'

The Lieutenant Harris and the Ensign Budd both shout out. 'Lovely angels!' they cry. 'Where did you come from?'

As for me, my tool rose, hardened to gigantic proportions in a single second.

The merchant smiles and nods his approval, when I translate their language of praise to him.

The two naked ones proceed to entertain us in the most lecherous manner. Now they advance to within a few feet of us. Then they retire swiftly backward.

Oh! How we all longed to seize them, and place our bursting pricks into their tight little slits!

Itsogoyu now says, 'They will tease you a while. Then I will fuck them both for your enjoyment.'

When I told this to my companions, they looked slightly disappointed.

'Where do we come in?' grumblingly speaks up the old Ned.

'Have no fear! You will soon have unexpected pleasures shown to you. Those stiff tools of yours will have such a shaking up that, before you are through, there will be nothing left of their hardness. Listen. Itsogoyu and myself are old cronies. We went to school together. We have had many a joyful time together. He is the finest fucker I ever knew. He is gifted with a prick that never falls in the presence of women. When a stiffness comes to him, it stays until he is through. He takes woman after woman without wilting it. He spends occasionally, but his penis remains as erect as when he begins.'

'Oh! He is certainly a lucky dog,' says the Lieutenant Harris.

'I would like to change pricks with him!' cries the old Ned, gazing at Itsogoyu in admiration. 'What! A hard-on all the time, and plenty of cunning little pussies to open! – Oh! Be Jaysus! I wish I was in his boots!'

Itsogoyu now becomes wild with lechery. He throws off his kimono. His fine prick stands out in splendid style. It looks like a rod of old yellow ivory. I can see the very veins in it swelling with the intensity of his hot and passionate desire.

The two Geishas still continue their fine dancing. One moment they show their plump arses. The next, they display all the beauties of their charming hairless slits. Now they embrace, fall upon the divans, and fuck each other furiously with their fingers. Then rising, they both advance to the merchant. Kneeling down beside him they fondle and kiss his tool in unison. Like a flash they are off again. They step behind the curtains for a moment, and then return, each with a bamboo switch in her hand. Now they chase one another, and bestow lively smarting blows on the dimpled cheeks of their arses.

Next Itsogoyu seizes a birch, and travels around the room in search of them. Pursuing them, he catches up with the laughing fairies, and bestows on each of them a not too delicate blow. As he does so, he pulls them to him; and, as if to atone for his cruelty, kisses the reddened spot a number of times.

'Heavens! What a glorious sight!' cries the Lieutenant Harris, holding his well-proportioned tool in control by his hand.

'Oh! Just God! Look at that other girl's slit!' cries the Ensign Budd, rapturously. 'See! Pearly drops are coming out of it! She is spending as she runs!'

'She will be the very first to be fucked,' I explain.

'God Almighty!' swears the old Ned. 'I could fuck that cunt for a week!'

'You may have a chance,' I say.

The girl who is spending now throws herself on the lounge and commences to work her arse wildly up and down.

'She wants a fucking badly!' I explain. 'And he will give it to her in fine style soon.'

I am right. The merchant does not fail to notice the invitation. He falls upon his knees, his stiff prick moving up and down in eager anticipation. Then he kisses her slit over and over again.

'I will fuck it hard, soon!' he cries out. 'Little angel, I will fuck it hard. Oh! How your arse will jump! – Won't it, you little angel? – Kiss your slit? Yes, darling! I will kiss it! – There! There! There! – That's it! Move your arse harder! Every one of those American gentlemen will fuck you when I get through with you. – You want them all? – You shall have them! I will open your slit for them! – But first let me kiss those pouting lips again! – There! There! There!'

The merchant grasps her by the cheeks of her arse, pushes her up until her jutting slit presents a most entrancing sight. We are all affected. The old Ned commences to dance a hornpipe, jerking himself off as he dances.

His example is contagious. My companions have lost control of themselves. I look about, and see the Lieutenant Harris and the Ensign Budd frantically engaged in jerking each other off.

As for me, I cannot restrain my dancing propensities. Around and around the room I go, slapping the blushing arse of the girl awaiting her turn, now bestowing upon Itsogoyu, as I pass, a blow that makes him thrust his ivory-colored rod deep into the amorous slit before him.

Away he goes, pumping his arse like an engine. The overjoyed girl beneath him quickly follows suit, and now both are busily engaged.

The remaining Geisha cries out in impatient lechery:

'Hurry up! – I burn! I burn!' And then she fairly moans in her sexual agony.

Then the Lieutenant Harris glances at me inquiringly.

THE MERCHANT ITSOGOYU

'Wait!' I answer. 'The merchant will be after her in a little while. He works so furiously that he fairly churns the cream within her. You can see it trickling down, so thick does it come from the Geisha. He can fuck for an hour yet and still have a stiff tool.'

Meanwhile, Itsogoyu is giving repeated lunges that stir her up. She shrieks. She cries with joy.

'Oh! Master, loose yourself!' she shouts. 'Pour into me the seed of life.'

As she speaks, he pulls forth his prick. Trickling drops fall from it, in whitish gouts upon the divan. He turns to me.

'Now, Lieutenant!' I cry. 'She is hot with desire! She wants a good load of hot semen to oil her inwardly. It is your turn to gratify her.'

In a second, the Lieutenant Harris is between her thighs. His noble prick enters with ease. He begins promptly to work his arse, and continues to thrust furiously into the heated slit.

Meanwhile the merchant is between the thighs of the waiting Geisha. He mumbles words of lustful love, and kisses and plays with her anxious slit. Then he pushes away at the tight little gates, and makes entrance with some difficulty. Her first cries of 'Oh! Oh! Oh!' give way to sighs of rapture when he is at length in.

The tool of the Lieutenant Harris is fairly bursting with pent up desires. He exchanges tongue kisses with the panting, crammed Geisha. At the same time he is fucking her in the most delightful manner.

'Let go! Let go!' the girl cries out. 'Pour it into me! Drown my womb with your oil of life. Pour it out! Now! – Else I will suck it out of you! – Noble Daimio! Dear Daimio! Tell him that I must have it – I am dying for it!'

'Let her have it, O most honourable Lieutenant!' I plead.

He answers with a furious lunge. Then he halts with his

almost bursting balls close against her skin. The girl gives a sigh of pleasure. Then I know that he is squirting it into her. Heave after heave she gives. At every one, another dose of sperm is ejected. By Iza! How their tongues work! I can see that they are enjoying themselves hugely.

'I say! Where do we come in?' shouts the Ensign Budd.

'Yes,' chimes in the old Ned. 'Where are we? Look at me prick! Ain't it a shame? – Ain't it? Say, Daimio, – there's nothing to take it! There ain't enough cunts to go round. God! How me balls aches!'

[Reader, I reproduce the man's language as it fell from his lips. Pardon me should its vulgarity fill your honourable mind with disgust. My purpose is to relate the facts of all our adventures in full.]

The merchant is seeking to satisfy the Geisha who had been waiting so long.

'Kind master!' she is crying. 'That thrust was most exquisite. Holy Buddha! You touch me to the very quick! – Ouch! Ouch! Let me roll on top of you!'

The merchant obeys the request, and soon the excited and delighted Geisha is bestriding him, working her lovely arse as fast as she is able.

'I know you cannot come off!' she shrieks. 'But I feel a loosening of the springs within me. – There! There! There! – I spend! – I – spend!'

Speaking thus, she moves her stomach spasmodically a number of times. Then she rolls off him and, loosening herself from his embrace, lies there panting and moving her stomach and arse convulsively, while the cream oozes in white gouts from her stretched and gaping little paradise of love.

Strange to say, the merchant rises, with penis well oiled, to be sure, but still as erect as when he first started.

THE MERCHANT ITSOGOYU

'Ha!' I cry. 'Look you, strangers from over the seas! Here is a prick that will not go down.'

Then I turn to the Ensign Budd, and point to the well-fucked girl who is still going through the motions which so lately had contributed to her pleasure.

'There! My boy, satisfy her!' I say.

He needs no second bidding. Like his companion he pauses not an instant. He glues himself to the lascivious Geisha. Quickly he inserts his swollen prick into her gaping, slippery cunt. The Geisha utters the most joyous cries. By the Gods! How I envied them the exquisite pleasure, for certainly it must be the superlative degree of enjoyment.

I expressed my thoughts aloud.

'If we were of the opposite sex, the highest pleasure we could have would be, to be fucked with a prick as stiff as the merchant's, and then to have another, equally as fine but juicier, pour its hot streams into a cunt burning with desire.'

'You bet your cock on that, old boy!' replied the old Ned, familiarly slapping me on the shoulders.

The merchant now retired to the bath. After sexual connection, it is customary for the people of Japan to cleanse themselves thoroughly.

'Water is the only thing that will take it down,' he remarked to the old Ned and myself. Then he added, 'Those girls are two of my best fuckers. They train for it. Being in my employ, they cater only to me. – Bah! They are not satisfied yet. – Your turn will come next.'

At this remark the old Ned hopped about with joy.

'It will be a wet deck, Daimy, but we will give it to them. You can bet your balls on it!'

'Tell me,' I inquired, 'why do you speak so strangely? I do not recall the words you mention.'

'Ha! Ha!' laughed he. 'Daimy, you are not up to snuff. A wet deck is a second-hand cunt, a box that some other fellow has just squirted into. Do you tumble?' Then he burst into a roar of laughter.

I turned to the two couples. The men were fucking the little angels as though they would split them apart. But, bless you! It only made the girls hotter with desire. Twice had the two Americans emptied their bags. Still the Geishas spurred them on. They played with their balls, fondled, caressed and kissed the shrunken tools, but they could not revive them.

Now suddenly one of the girls looks at me.

'Oh! Look at the Daimio's thick thing!' she cries. 'Oh! I want it! I want it!'

'You shall not have it!' exclaims the other, seeking to hold her back.

In a short space of time she was mine.

As I seize her I cry, 'I will kiss and kiss this well-fucked slit. – Oh! Haunt of delight! House of never-failing joy! – Oh! Lovely ruby-lined treasure spot! – I will fuck you with this hardened prick until your shrieks are loud and long. Oh! I would fuck you on the springing divan in the corner – out in the niches of the hall – up and down the stairs, in the by-ways. Yes, all through the house will I fuck you.'

Saying this, I bestowed fervid kisses on the moist lips of her pouting slit. Oh! Gods! How I fondled it! Then I pushed my teeming prick into the velvet passage, fucked my way despite her cries until my balls rattled loosely against her arse-hole. Joining her lips to mine, clasping my hands around the dimpled cheeks of her splendid arse, I started on my journey. I darted about frantically. Then we fell into a corner, where I pumped her furiously. Next we were in the

The Merchant Itsogoyu

hall, where I bounded into the air. I rested her in an alcove, and again worked my arse with all my power. This brought on the shrieking. Her shrill cries were as music in my ears. My lips were between her teeth.

Into another apartment did we go. There, on a couch, I commenced to work again. A fine stream came from me. Yet still harder grew my prick. I placed her on the stairs, and fucked and fucked away. Another stream caused her to shriek with renewed fervour. I placed my tongue down her throat, and still fucking, now and then ramming her plump arse against the wall, I ran through the house, up and down the stairs, and at length carried her back to the apartment where we had begun.

As I entered, old Ned was fiercely fucking the other Geisha, who appeared to greatly enjoy his fierce, wild, powerful lunges.

'Ho! Girlee! Girlee! – Oh! But you're good!' shouted out the pleased old salt. 'I will squirt a quart in you, soon! – Ouch! Don't bite! – You little bitch, take your teeth out! – Do you hear? Be Jaysus! I will give it to you! – There! Take that! And that! – There! – Take-to-a-at! – Jaysus! How I am squirting! – Hey! But I have got another hard-on! – Now, girlee! Girlee! I am off again! – Get up, boy! Get up! It's a haydiddle-diddle, and a hey-diddle-diddle, and a whoop-de-dooden-do! – Oh! Oh! Oh! I squirt again! I'm off! – There! – Be God! Get out of here! I've had enough of you! – I ain't no hog!'

During this proceeding I was in the seventh heaven of delight. I lay down and pressed my Geisha close to me. Without moving, I poured into her overheated slit a perfect stream of the juice she loved.

This was too much for her. She fell off of me, rolled over

and over and then lay quiet. A slight quivering of her arse indicated the state of ecstasy she was in.

The merchant, who had returned to the apartment, laughed heartily at the sight.

'O San (honourable miss),' he remarked sarcastically, 'often to me hast you complained of my want of sexual juice. Now – Ha! Ha! – You art gorged like an overfed pig. Most noble companions, look! The semen is running from her yet.'

Itsogoyu spoke the truth. The Geisha, sick with joy, was moving her arse still. At each move she would eject semen.

'She is a priceless gem,' said the merchant. 'The Mikado himself has had his eyes upon her.'

'Ho!' I cried. 'She is a fit mate for him. By all our gods! I swear 'tis hard to find her equal.'

The Ensign Budd valiantly spoke up in defense of the other.

'I never tasted such a dainty dish,' he said. 'By Heaven! Thought I would never get enough. Good friend,' he continued, turning to Itsogoyu, 'the women of Japan are the most tempting pieces of flesh ever served up to a man with such a cast-iron hard-on as your dishes have given us.'

The old Ned as usual, had a say.

'Right you are, Mr Ensign!' he cried. Then turning to me, he added, 'Daimy, old boy! – That young cunt was as fine as silk! – Lord! How I did work my arse! – Oh! But won't I have hard-on stories to tell when I get back home?'

Itsogoyu now informed us that the bath was awaiting our pleasure. We all retired to enjoy a soothing plunge in warm, perfumed waters, where we disported like so many fish.

After we emerged, we returned to the banquet-room, where an elegant repast was spread for us. We were all, however, too thoroughly tired out to derive further enjoyment from the pleasures of appetite. One by one the heads began to nod around the board. We fell asleep over our cups, and were presently assisted to our respective apartments.

IV
A ROYAL BRIDAL NIGHT

The next few days were given over to sightseeing. The merchant was our chaperon. We spent some afternoons in going around Kyoto. To many of you I am sure it will be as wonderful a city, as it was to my American friends.

Here can be seen the great Buddhist temple, which is not yet completed. The whole of the temple, with its immense curved roof of vast proportions, its marvellous wood carvings, has been built by offerings of labour, money and materials contributed by the faithful. The magnificent buildings that surround it, the stores crowded with the most elegant specimens of Japanese handiwork, and numerous other attractions, all excited the admiration and the wonder of my American friends.

But most interesting to us all were the tea-houses, great and small inns, cook-shops which were mainly houses of prostitution as well as of accommodation. Courtesans, dressed and perfumed, came out about the noon-hour. Standing at the door, or sitting upon a small gallery, they boldly solicit customers. What smiles and signals were given us! How tempting a sight it was! The old Ned could not restrain himself.

'Look at that handsome bitch over there!' he shouted, pointing to a plump and pretty girl who was making signals with her stomach to us. 'Oh! Be God!' he cried. 'She's a fucker from base. Oh! Look at it! – Say, masters, let's get out. I want a piece of that!'

Itsogoyu frowned severely when I tried to translate these remarks. The phrase. 'A piece of that,' was beyond my power of expressing. I inquired of the Lieutenant Harris what its meaning was. He laughingly informed me.

The merchant gravely rebuked us.

'When a woman suits our taste,' he said, 'we have her examined and sent to our abode. It would be a severe reflection upon me for any one of my guests to be seen entering these houses. If the sailor desires the woman so strongly, I will have her sent to my house.'

This kind offer was mentioned to the old Ned, who was greatly affected by the liberality of our host.

'Thank your honour kindly,' he replied, touching his hat. 'I just had a fancy for her – that's all. But I was only a-foolin'. What! Me? – Me? – Me get into that stale cunt after what I have just had? – Nix-e-e! Why I wouldn't touch it with a ten-foot pole.'

We were now informed that the question of our proper entertainment had been a source of much solicitude to the merchant. The question of expense was not even a moment's consideration with him.

'I have,' said he, 'engaged a corps of actors who cater to the wealthy and noble. They will perform for you, to-morrow evening, the play of the *Mikado's Daughter, or the Royal Bridal Night*. The subject of the play dates back a few centuries, and will treat of the love of the daughter of a Mikado for a young noble, and its happy termination. You must know that, for the most part, the daughters of our Emperors were not permitted to marry. Everyone was esteemed beneath them. I will tell you no more, save that

A Royal Bridal Night

you will enjoy the most lecherous feast that has ever been your lot to partake of.'

When I told this to my hearers, the most noble Americans, they were greatly pleased thereat.

At the time appointed, we all assembled in the private theatre, situated in the upper portions of Itsogoyu's magnificent residence. The superb climate of Japan (the same as that of Heaven) would alone account for such an exhibition. The roof had been removed, and the stars became plainly visible.

We sat in the midst of luxurious foliage. The stage was surrounded in a similar manner.

Itsogoyu had invited several of his closest friends. One of these, we were told, was a Kuge or count – next in rank to imperial princes. Another was a Go-Inkyo-Sama or retired gentleman.

The Japanese, I would have you know, are extremely fond of the play-house. They patronize it freely, and find it a great source of entertainment. The subjects of their plays have more or less reference to the heroic deeds of their forefathers, and in their plays is illustrated some unheard-of sacrifice, or terrible trial of endurance. Again the play will touch upon the passion of love, and depict it in all its varied phases.

It is my intention, courteous reader, to present to you a play teeming with the most voluptuous pleasure. Fail not to attend closely, and you will be amply repaid. Come, participate with me. I invite your presence at the feast.

The first scene is in the boudoir of Nolinga, the Mikado's daughter, who is reposing on a divan, surrounded by her maids of honour. Enter six rosy-cheeked youths who are covered with leaves. They dance before the ladies. Presently they throw off their leafy covering and appear entirely nude. Their performances become wildly lecherous. They play with and fondle one another until their fine young tools become large and stiff. At this stage, six beautiful young maidens enter. The youths retire to the background. Then the maidens begin to dance in the most graceful and entrancing manner, their coloured kimonos making a delightfully varied kaleidoscopic picture. Finally they throw off every bit of their coverings, and show to all their secret beauties. They taunt and tease the males – now advancing then retreating.

Another signal is given. A couch is placed before Nolinga. A youth and a maiden lock arms. The maid is then placed in the most entrancing position. A little cushion is placed beneath her dimpled arse. Her lovely slit is uppermost.

The youth flushes rosy red at the sight. He presses kisses on her entire body. Then he halts and gazes in unspeakable admiration at the hairless treasure.

Nolinga laughs heartily and says:

'Fortunate boy! What would you say if now I commanded you to depart under penalty of losing your life?'

'Most mighty mistress,' returns the youth, 'humbly I would reply, "Deprive me not of this heavenly pleasure. Let me just pierce those precious lips with my throbbing staff of love. – Then take my life if you will." '

The old Ned, as usual, has to interject his remarks.

'What! Leave that? – Hey! – Leave it! – By Christ! I wouldn't leave it if they cut me cock off the next moment! – Come, boy! – Work your ass! Work your ass! I want to see you squirt!'

The Lieutenant Harris was highly indignant at this

A ROYAL BRIDAL NIGHT

untoward interruption. He bestowed upon the old Ned a resounding kick.

'That's right, Lieutenant. That's right!' spoke up the old Ned. 'Kick me ass! – Kick it again! – I ought to ha' kept me mouth shut.'

The company on the stage, having recovered their composure, proceed.

The youth places his tool between the jutting lips and gives a fierce lunge. The girl cries out. He continues with a second push. His balls rest against her arse. She squirms with mingled pain and delight.

Now the other dancers form a ring and begin a chant.

> Behold the lovers in close embrace!
> Mark their gesturings, their kissings!
> Now hear the plaintive maid's entreaties!
> Yea, hear her mockings: she speaks not truth.
> His staff has pierced her to the full!
> Untold treasures would not relax her grasp.
> So close she clings he scarce can breathe.
> And now together they are as one,
> Unconscious of all else about them.
> The quivering staff of love's bedewed.
> See, from its sheath he pulls it outwards.
> Then swiftly flying back into her
> It finds her as eager as before.
> Glorious Amida! Fully bless them!
> Prolong their rapturous bliss forever.
> Now joy complete comes hastening onward.
> See, their forms are all a-trembling.
> Forth the seed flows, is sucked upwards,
> Into the greedy waiting womb.

Now come the cries, the sighs of pleasure,
Till passion cools within the youth.
The maid is burning with fierce desire
Her kissings devour him, her voice
In tones solicitous and trembling
Throughout the hall is heard.

'Once more! – Dear love!' she cries. 'Once more! My very entrails burn! I am all aflame! Oh! Quench the fire within me!'

The youths and the maidens cease their song. The partly-satisfied actors are now thrust aside. Another couple take their place and engage in the sexual combat, with an appetite whetted by long waiting.

'What a delightful play,' whispers the Lieutenant Harris in my ear.

' 'Tis but the beginning!' I return. 'Hold yourself in abeyance for what is to follow.'

The youth is troubled to find entrance into the tightened slit before him. See! The maiden rises. Now she bends her body and licks his fine tool until it is slippery with her saliva. Now he returns it to the tight little cavern of delight.

As he enters it more easily, a maiden falls behind him with her arms closely pressed around his loins. Her throbbing breasts quiver against his broad back. She, in turn, is embraced by another of the youths. The others follow in rotation, and we can plainly see the eager pricks knocking furiously at the entrances to the burning slits.

'It's a game of back-scuttle!' hoarsely whispers the old Ned.

* * *

The fucking is now perfectly grand. As the one on the couch draws back, the rest all follow. Then five swollen pricks are tightly encased in five cunning pouting slits. Now they commence to sing, keeping time with the music of the sexual organs.

(The Ensign Budd tells me, kind reader, that this is a pun. I am sure it is an unconscious one, and so I crave thy considerate indulgence for the mishap.)

As they sing, they increase their movements.

Oh! Immortal Gods! What a sight it is! The Mikado's daughter throws aside her rich habiliments and presents to our view a most glorious specimen of naked womanhood.

'Oh! What an entrancing scene is this!' she cries, running round and about, peering between their thighs, watching the long line moving forward and backward, first slowly, then quickly.

'Oh! Rapture! Rapture!' she cries. 'Fit beginning of my bridal night!'

Then the lovely being falls backward, her eager slit uppermost, whilst a maid plays vigorously with her excited clitoris. Soon she, too, is keeping time with the rest, and working her arse as ecstatically as any of the others.

The actress who assumed the part of the Mikado's daughter was a most beautiful woman. Her long black hair was loosened and fell to the floor when she stood upright. The rounded hemispheres on her breast were hard, and tipped with nipples as bright and firm as priceless rubies. Her stomach was not too full, but just sufficiently plump to excite one to distraction. Her firm thighs and rounded ankles would have made the fortune of a sculptor. But the greatest of all her treasures was the superb slit. One would scarcely believe its lips had ever been parted. At the top of the slit the jutting lips raised themselves in dimpled beauty. Along the sides the vermilion was plainly visible.

'The Mikado was the first to fuck her,' I whispered. 'It takes a fortune to enjoy this woman. Ah! But she is in splendid condition. You will shortly witness a sight that will excel in exciting scenes anything that you have previously come in contact with.'

I had no listeners. All eyes were fixed upon the stage.

The long line of excited men and women forget the parts they are enacting. They are human now. See! How uniformly the stiff tools of the youths are working. Every slit wants all it can get. Some seek more. The quivering arses are eager to express themselves. As the pleasure becomes greater, their movements increase. Even the girl playing with her mistress's clitoris moves her arm in unison with the rest. They are all fucking with might and main. Pricks and arses are working furiously.

Some of the maidens utter little shrieks. Others sigh deeply. Their breasts heave with pleasure. The men utter a simultaneous cry. Their balls touch their partners' arseholes. They breathe heavily, and quiver like reeds in a storm.

'Ah! They are spending!' shouts Itsogoyu, greatly excited by the sight.

He is right. It is plain to be seen by the joyful expressions on the faces of the participants that the crisis has arrived.

The old Ned cannot contain himself.

'Let her go, boys! Let her go!' he shouts. 'Squirt into 'em like hell! – Oh! They want it bad! – That's the way! Make

A ROYAL BRIDAL NIGHT

'em jump! – Hey! Hey! I've got a spare cock! Who wants it?'

For a reply he receives a kick in the arse from the indignant Lieutenant Harris, whilst the Ensign Budd gives him a cuff over the ear. This effectually silences him.

Some of the maidens now throw themselves flat upon the floor, and repeatedly raise their arses up and down. Others chases one another about the stage.

The Mikado's daughter has spent freely with the rest, and lies on the couch, her arse trembling with pleasure.

'A good stiff tool would be very appropriate for her now,' observes the retired merchant.

'She will have one soon,' replies Itsoguyu.

The bell now rings, and all but the principal actors leave the stage.

A maid briskly sponges off the mistress. She resumes her attire, and bids her attendants to retire. Then she speaks thus:

'This is my bridal night. Long have I waited for this festal time. I now shall have my fill of sexual delight. I am fairly burning with desire. I must be granted supreme satisfaction, else I shall be consumed by the fierce fires of my lust.

'Know that my lover is the Prince Katouka, Son of the deposed Tycoon. Our families have sworn eternal enmity, but what care we for their quarrelings? We love! We peril all to obtain one another! A disgraceful death awaits the discovery of our union. To-night we will revel in pleasure – to-morrow we may pay the penalty. I command you to commence the festivities. Every minute will be crowded with bliss. Time therefore is precious beyond riches.'

Then she strides forward and turning, addresses us.

'Most noble gentlemen, this is the first act of our play. I crave your merciful favour for what is lacking. Have patience. There are in store for you amorous surprises that will please you greatly.'

With these words she bows her head to the floor. Then the curtain falls and the first act is over.

V
THE HOUR OF THE ROSE

Previous to the commencement of the second and last act in the drama, we were served with and partook of refreshments. Dainty dishes, fit for a monarch's palate, gave place to the choicest champagne, of which we all drank copiously. The night, though warm, was tempered by a cooling breeze.

We chatted pleasantly among ourselves.

'I cannot express to you, noble friend,' observes the Lieutenant Harris, 'the delight we all feel. Our enjoyment is beyond our power of expression.'

'I echo the words of my friend,' adds the Ensign Budd, 'and must say that nothing could in any way add to our pleasure. I trust you will express our sentiments and gratitude to our genial host.'

'I'm in it, too,' observes the old Ned. 'This is the finest thing I ever struck. Say!' he added in a hoarse whisper. 'All we want when this here play is over is a fine young cunt piece, something juicy, a nice little tight slit. – Whoop! Whoop!' he shouts. 'But wouldn't I fuck it!'

'Have no fear,' I reply. 'Itsogoyu always anticipates all the wants of his guests. We will be well provided for.'

We next listened to a musical interlude played on the Koto (a cross between a piano and a harp, as Ensign Budd is pleased to explain it). The musician was not visible, but its tones were soft and soothing at first, – then rose to upper notes loud and stirring. An attendant came out and placed in position a Kakemono (a hanging scroll on which was written what at first we took to be a description of the next act of the play). Judge of our surprise when I read as follows, translating as I went, that my American friends might be as fully informed:

> The honourable and most highly respected merchant Itsogoyu, renowned as the possessor of great riches, the supporter of the throne, who refusing from his grateful master all titles of honour whatsoever, is content to be known throughout the length and breadth of the Empire as the Generous Giver. Let it be placed in letters of gold over his door, 'No one deserving of charity appealeth to him in vain.'
>
> *By order of*
> THE EMPEROR.

When I had translated this, the noble Americans joined with me in loud applause. The merchant modestly received our expressions of approbation. Then the signal given, the play proceeded.

The scene opens with a view of the bridal chamber, which is furnished in the most luxurious manner. The couch is covered with a silken cloth decorated with gold and silver flowers. The rug is the most superb specimen of Japanese handicraft, and the furnishings generally are all of the most expensive kind.

A maid enters, and proceeds to arrange the bed for its occupation. A few moments later, a merry troop of lovely maidens enter in company with the blushing bride. They exchange jests with one another.

'Ha! Ha!' laughs a fair punster. 'You knowest that dagger plunged into its sheath is harmless. Remember, you wilt be pierced this night, and your soft sheath wilt receive its proper weapon.'

' 'Tis the after result must be feared,' speaks up another.

'You are all envious of me,' answers the bride quickly. 'Come! Prepare me! – I am tired of these jestings.'

The maidens utter little shouts of delight as they remove the virgin's apparel.

'Oh! What a lovely bosom!' cries one, as she uncovers the small rounded globes. 'Would that I were a man, that I might suck those ruby tips!'

Saying which, she greedily places her mouth to a rosy nipple, and seeks to gather its sweets.

'Such arms and back!' chimes in another.

'And such arse and thighs!' adds a third.

'Oh! Behold this splendid badge of womanhood!' exclaims the first speaker. 'Has not she a treasure! See me press the jutting lips! It is like fine satin! – Let me arouse all her passions! – I will play with her clitoris.'

'I will! I will! Let me!' exclaim several others.

'The bridegroom is waiting,' pleads a voice in the corridor.

'Bid him wait. All the night is his!' was the answer.

The maidens are filled with lechery. Two dainty little fingers from different hands are inserted in the tight slit. They play vigorously.

The pleased bride commences to work her arse slowly. Then as the busy fingers titillate her, she moves herself up and down in the most delightful and entrancing manner.

* * *

'Holy Moses!' observes the old Ned. 'How I would like to be on top of that! – Oh! It's tough! Damn tough! – Ah! Ah! Ah! – Nice little cunny! Oh! Oh! How I would like to fuck it hard! – Yum! Yum! – I must hold me prick hard! Yum! Yum! Yum! – Jaysus! I've gone off in my pants! – Ah! I feel better now!'

A severe look from the Lieutenant Harris causes the old salt to subside.

'Have done in there!' cries a commanding voice. 'I tell you the bridegroom is wild with impatience!'

'Oh! Finish it first!' pleads the bride. 'Do not leave me yet! – Ah! Ah! Oh! – Further down! – Ah! Ah! Ah! – Further up! That's the place, girls! – Oh! That is elegant! Ah! Ah! Ah! – I am coming!'

Saying which the pleased bride frantically moves her arse with such force that the maidens are powerless.

'Let us away!' cries one. 'For she is well prepared to receive the bridegroom!'

With this the group of smiling girls departs.

The last speaker had spoken truthfully. Modesty was thrown to the winds. The bride lay perfectly naked. Her thighs were extended, her feet just touching the floor. One of the maids had spread a soft pillow under her posteriors. This caused her beautiful slit to stand out in a manner sufficient to set a man crazy with lust.

She sings softly:

> Come! Beloved, come!
> I eagerly await thee!
> Thou hast that which alone
> Is all that will sate me.
> Long I've been denied –

> Quickly come, I pray thee!
> Let me be satisfied –
> Oh! Love, do not delay me.

The next instant the bridegroom enters.

'Oh! Lovely one!' he cries. 'You are indeed prepared for me! My Nolinga, I will soon be in your arms.'

Speaking thus, he discards his apparel, with astonishing rapidity, and in an instant more he is kneeling stark naked at her feet.

He is a robust fellow, strong and supple of limb. As he turns his back you can see the play of the fine muscles. When he shows his front he is a glorious sight. His breasts are plump, his thighs massive. Between them is a right royal prick – thick and vigorous in appearance. Heavy balls display themselves beneath the instrument of love.

The bride gazes at it with eager eyes. She is wild to obtain it. See! He falls down between her thighs and kisses the dewy lips of her slit again and again. At each kiss she gives a gentle heave. Her hands are frantically moving themselves in search of his tool.

Then he begins a chant:

> Oh! Light of my soul!
> How eagerly have I thought of you!
> Your hidden beauties have nigh undone me!
> Oft have I dreamt that these lovely lips
> Have oped themselves to my swelling arrow.
> A thousand times, in my imagination,
> Have I pierced you to the very quick!
> Yet a thousand times again
> I've thought of you thus reclining –
> I've lulled myself to sleep

With thoughts of you lying thus.
Madly I love! I risk death to obtain you;
Now comes the hour of triumph at hand.
I shall consummate all my fond desires.

As he ceases he clasps her body in his arms.

'There, beloved one, press this stiffened staff.'

She madly seizes it, and with little cries of lechery voices her satisfaction as she rubs its stiffened length with her dainty hand. Now see! How eagerly she presses his tool! Her other hand weighs his well-hung balls, and plays with and fondles the elastic things.

'This is the finest play I ever witnessed,' remarked the Ensign Budd to me in a whisper. 'If it were in the States,' he continued, 'no theatre would be large enough to hold the people.'

'Superb! Superb!' was what the Lieutenant Harris remarked.

I noticed that his lengthy tool was fairly running away. His two hands were pressed hard upon it. My own caused me feel the most pleasant sensations. I could feel little drops coming from me, at intervals. I was slowly spending.

'Daimy,' said the old Ned. 'This play takes the cake! – Good Lord! I hope it will last all night! – Say,' he whispered loudly. 'Haven't you a spare cunt about? I am awful ornery. – Jesus! But I would like to pump away at that ere girl's slit! – I've got to go out for a little. 'Scuse me, Daimy, while I go piss – will you?'

I did not heed his further remarks. I heard something like this:

'. . . will have a quiet little jerk all to myself! . . . Wish I had a cunt, though! Oh! Wouldn't I? . . .' and so on.

* * *

The bridegroom becomes so greatly excited by the bride's fondling of him that he moves uneasily. She is working his thick prick most vigorously. His finger is buried in her burning slit, until she can stand it no longer. See! She fairly pulls him on top of her. The head of his tool opens the lips that speak mutely of paradise beyond. A move of his arse places the head of his penis in completely.

The bride's tongue hangs out and wags like the tail of a kite. He fights it with his own tongue, moving his buttocks with swift and powerful strokes.

'Oh! Gods! It must be fine!' cries out Itsogoyu. 'Ho! There! – Are you acting, or is this reality?'

The bridegroom withdraws himself from the bride's embraces, solemnly marches to the front of the stage, and shaking his prick before our eyes he returns this answer:

'Pardon my boldness! Look at this!'

Speaking thus he again shakes his stiff tool at us.

'Call you it acting? The sight of so much magnificent beauty lying so temptingly naked before one would rouse even a corpse! No! No! This is real. We cannot manufacture hard-ons to order.'

With another bow, he hastens to his partner. He places his staff once again into her waiting slit, and works with redoubled zeal. She joins her arms about his neck. She clasps her legs about his back, and holds him close for a short period. Their mouths exchange tongues. Now his arse begins to move. It works more swiftly than before. Now he is pumping away at her at a rapid rate.

A shrill scream comes from the delighted girl.

'Oh! It's so heavenly!' she cries. 'Ah! Ah! – Give it to me harder! – That's good! That's sweet! – Suck my tongue! – There! There! I come! I come! – Oh! Oh! Oh! I feel a burning stream! – Now one long sweet kiss! Then come again!'

His arse moves convulsively. He squirts a heavy stream into her this time, and then withdraws his conquered tool, as if reluctant to leave his paradise.

The merchant makes a gesture. The satisfied lover takes the hint and retires.

Nolinga is unconscious of his departure. She turns herself face downward on the couch, and slowly moves herself up and down. The voluptuous girl, gorged and crammed with delight, is quivering with the excess of pleasure she has just received.

Presently the gong is sounded. The maids re-enter and cover the Princess with flowers. A full-blown rose is placed daintily over her pretty slit.

'I thought we would have a little fun, gentlemen,' remarked the merchant. 'The play is done. Now select your ladies and enjoy them to your heart's content. But I beg of you to hold in remembrance the fact that the actress who has played the part of the Princess is reserved for myself.'

'I see a cunt-piece that I want,' cries the old Ned. Saying which he caught hold of a girl who was the oldest of the crowd.

The Lieutenant Harris soon had a dainty little witch in his arms and was hard at work stripping her to nakedness. The Ensign Budd was similarly employed.

The remaining three were now left to the merchant's friends and myself.

The merchant quickly disrobes, and kneels between the actress's thighs. His noble prick is standing up in fine style. He removes the full blown rose that hid the pouting lips.

Then he plays with her treasure-casket, and calls it by a thousand endearing names. For a while he teases it with the stiffened head of his prick. She moves her arse from side to side. Then he gives a sudden lunge that causes her to gasp for breath, and buries his tool deep in her. She seeks to work, but he will not permit it. His head reposes on her bosom, which heaves and swells with the exquisite pleasure.

'I will not move till I spend!' he says, drawing her still closer to him.

The crammed girl is in the seventh heaven of bliss. She has what she wants now.

Meanwhile the Lieutenant Harris and the Ensign Budd are playing with their partners' slits. The girls open their thighs as if to bid for further pleasure.

The old Ned has no time for preliminaries. He has placed his partner on the cushion, with her legs up in the air, and his bull-headed prick is making her jump like an athlete.

'No jack-ass about this, shouts the old Ned. 'There! Girlee, work your ass again!

'– Ah! That's the ticket! Now don't come yet, for I'm not ready – Phew! I smell the Jack's fart yet. He must be rotten! – Say, girlee, you're all right! Oh! This is rich! – Ouch! Don't come, you devil! – Ah! You've squirted all over me, you bitch! – Gee! whoop! I can't hold it back much longer! There! I'm off! Feel the squirt? You bet your ass you do!'

[Really this farrago of nonsense should not be repeated to you, reader. Had I not promised to faithfully relate all the occurrences of our memorable pleasure trip. I should avoid giving space to the old Ned's quaint phraseology.]

My own selection was unusually choice. She was a seventeen-year-old from the mountain district. Taught the pleasure of love at an early age, she was now an adept.

I was soon playing with her moist love passage. It was soft as velvet to my touch. She squirmed and twisted as my finger probed her preparatory to my inserting the proper instrument that women long for.

'I want to be fucked bad,' she whispered between her sighs and kisses. 'But first set me going. Rub me, master.'

I soon 'set her going', for her arse quivered like a maple leaf in the wind.

'Oh! Excellency,' she cries. 'You touch me to the very heart! – My! What a thick tool you have! Shall I work it like this?'

And then she worked it until it was rigid as a bar of iron in its stiffness.

'Darling little one! Your slit is dying for it. There, now! You spend! – I will work you further up. – Ho! Ho! You spend again! – I will soon put my swelling prick in there and stop that leak! It's tight and wet in there, isn't it, little darling? My prick is almost bursting! We will dance a little!'

With this I mount her and work my tool completely in. As the soft clinging walls of her hall of lecherous pleasure yield before my onward pushings, the head of my stiffened tool is most delightfully caressed and titillated. She fits me like a tight glove. My ponderous engine straightens out every wrinkle of her clinging nook of paradise. Then I seize the cheeks of her arse, and as she tightly hugs me, I get a good firm grasp of her dimpled backside and carry her about the apartment. This, as the reader has already been informed, is my favourite method.

What a luscious fuck it was! My excited partner commenced to sing one of our most admired ballads. She told me afterwards that when a man's tool was encased in her, she always sang in this manner. (She's not the only one I've made to sing with my big tool.)

> Shosumi the fair, your lovely eyes
> Outshine the blue and cloudless skies.
> Your scarlet lips and silken hair
> And graceful form beyond compare
> Cause me to love you deeply,
> Cause me to love you dearly.

As she finished this first verse, I poured into her womb a copious flow that made her cease singing.

I remove my prick to the tip, then jump with her into the air, and push it back at one swift stroke. My gyrations are wonderful to behold. I even succeed in throwing a somersault in the air, she clinging closely to me all the while, to the great wonder and astonishment of everyone.

I give another squirt that enters her very vitals. Then away I race, treading on prostrate forms regardlessly. I place the pleased, and gorged, and crammed girl on a couch, and begin to work in and out, in and out until she shrieks, moans and sobs with pleasure.

'I will finish now, darling one,' I cry loudly. 'Now! One more shove! There! – Yet another! And another! There! My balls are against your arse. Fuck my tongue! – That is delicious! – There! There! There! I am off again! Now, sweet one, we will rest thus!'

'Look at the Daimy!' cries the old Ned. 'He ain't through yet. Say, old boy, we are all pumped out! Even Itsogoyu, too. He ain't got any hard-on. Come, get off! We're hungry, I've had enough cunt for a while.'

I withdrew myself from my partner, and joined the rest.

The girls now left us. We retired to the bath, and for an hour lingered there. Refreshed by our ablutions we gathered around the banquet table, where we all did ample justice to the delicacies provided for us by our generous host. After which we all drank champagne until we sank into sweet oblivion.

VI
OUCH!

During the next month, my friend the merchant exhausted all the pleasures of Kyoto to please us. We were the principal participants in numerous banquets. Tea-shops, theatres, gambling houses were all in turn visited and enjoyed. That most fascinating ballet, the Miyaki-Odori afforded us all intense pleasure. The fine women who composed the ballet were the most beautiful that I ever beheld. The Lieutenant Harris and the Ensign Budd were loud in their praises.

The merchant, with his usual prodigality, had secured very desirable seats, thus affording us a close view of the dances.

The ballet was lechery disguised in the similitude of virtue. Every one of the dancers was an accomplished fucker, capable of giving one the most intense enjoyment.

The old Ned became so excited as to be at times beyond control.

'Oh! Jesus!' he cried. 'Look at the one with her belly moving as if she had stiff prick stuck in her. – Say, I can't keep me cock down. – Oh! Girlee! How I would like to squeeze your lemon! – Ouch! Look at that! Be God! if she does that again I'll jump on the stage and fuck her before the whole crowd!'

Fearing that he might be tempted to commit an overt act,

STATES OF ECSTASY

and also noting that his conduct was beginning to attract the attention of the audience, we forced him into the background where he remained comparatively quiet.

We enjoyed ourselves in this manner for upwards of a month. Religious festivals, fetes, gymnastic exercises and what not were in turn exhausted.

'It is getting time to fuck again,' I said to the noble Americans. 'Then too,' I added, 'we have enjoyed the merchant's hospitality to an unbounded extent. I for one am not willing to trench upon it longer.'

'Nor will we,' said the two officers simultaneously.

'What the boss says is law,' chimes in the old Ned.

'Listen,' I continued. 'The Kuge has spoken to me privately, and states that he is going to open his country mansion to-morrow. He extends to you through me a cordial invitation to enjoy his hospitality, and promises to give us an orgy that will exceed anything that you have ever witnessed.'

The old Ned jumped a foot or more in the air as an expression of his delight, while the Lieutenant Harris and the Ensign Budd expressed their pleasure in their faces.

'Remember, most excellent sir,' said the Lieutenant Harris, 'that our leave of absence expires with the month. Ere it has passed, we must report at Yokohama. Therefore, lose no time. Every hour is now precious to us.'

I obeyed his request. A few short hours, and three jinrikishas were waiting to transport us to Nagaike. The merchant accompanied us. Our solicitations had so strongly appealed to him that he could not resist them.

Upon our arrival at the Kuge's mansion, I was attracted by the voice of the old Ned. It was pitched in a louder key than usual.

'Damn the infernal luck, Daimy! I can't get me boot off! Can't I hop into the house?'

OUCH!

Now it is well known that in Japan no one enters a house with his boots on. Of course, you are aware, that they are removed and replaced by soft felt slippers. One might as well in your own country attempt to walk on the tables and chairs as to enter a Japanese residence with boots or shoes on.

Without waiting to suggest a remedy I took out my pocket-knife and cut the boot apart, thus removing it with ease.

As I turned to enter I heard the following:

'Well, I'm damned! What in hell do you take me for, Daimy, anyhow? – One of them Vanderbilts, or Rothschilds? – Why, Daimy, them 'ere boots is new! How in hell will I get another pair! Je-sus! Who in hell's a-kicking me ass? – Oh! It's you, Lieutenant? Well, it's all right. I won't say another word.'

After an enjoyable bath, we sat down to a most tempting banquet. The dishes were indeed appetizing, and the wines exquisite. At the end of two hours we reposed idly in our seats and enjoyed fragrant Manillas.

I suppose, courteous reader, that after a good dinner, you have felt as we did. Our stomachs were full and our passions excited. I felt my prick steadily rising. I saw also that the Lieutenant Harris and the Ensign Budd moved their arses about uneasily.

As usual, the old Ned voiced our sentiments in his peculiar coarse way.

'Wish I had a cunt to play with,' says he. 'I'd like to pinch and fumble, and run me hand around, and see her ass jump. A nice tight cunt would go first rate, eh, Daimy, old boy?'

Hardly had he uttered the words, than the hangings were thrust aside and six pert little misses entered and presented themselves before us.

'What have we here, Saigo?' inquires the merchant.

[I forgot to inform you that Saigo was the name of the Kuge. Henceforth, reader, you will understand when I speak of him by name.]

Saigo smiled.

'I have something which I am positive you all desire, and that is cunt.'

We all shout approval.

The maidens arise, and each in turn comes to one of us, climbs upon our laps, throws open her kimono, and shows us her naked beauties.

'Oh! Jizo! What luck!' I cry.

Then I examine my prize. She is a little beauty of seventeen, with skin like satin. Her titties show themselves fine, while her plump round stomach, and rounded thighs make my prick fairly jump into stiffness. Then she opens her legs and shows me her slit.

'Oh! Angel!' I shout. 'What a sweet-darling thing you have! How nice it will be to play with it! – But look at my thick prick!' I add, removing my kimono. 'How like you that?'

'Master, it is fine,' she returns, with a lecherous gleam in her eyes.

I pinched the soft lips of her hairless slit. Then I inserted my fingers and lay back, and gently played with her clitoris. She grasps my prick and proceeds to work the throbbing thing.

'Softly, angel!' I cry. 'Just work me gently. See how slowly I play with you. We must make this last for a while.'

I threw off her kimono, and placed my arm around her naked form, and held her closely to me.

She had a round face and black eyes. She possessed crimson-tinged cheeks, downy like the ripened momo (peach). Her long black hair fell in strands of jet down her back. Her coral mouth was small but ripe and when its lips opened, small, even rows of white teeth displayed themselves.

'Companions,' cried Saigo, 'these are selected beauties, fit for a Mikado.'

'Every one costs a small fortune to secure, I warrant you,' speaks up Itsogoyu.

'Oh! This is a perfect treasure that I have,' interjects the delighted Lieutenant Harris.

'As for me,' observes the Ensign Budd, 'I cannot find words to express my gratification.'

'Ha! Ha!' I cry. 'We have cunts worth fortunes. I for one would not part with mine for a mint of money.'

As for the old Ned, he was wrapped up in his charmer.

'There! Sissy, don't jerk so hard! Me prick won't stand it! First thing I know, I will squirt on you! – Do you hear, you little bitch? – My! What a juicy cunt you have! – There! I'll tickle you further up! How's that, Sissy? Oh! You feel it, do you? Ouch! – See here! You'll pull me prick out! – Don't work so fast! I ain't so young as I used to be! – I tell you, Sis, that one time I was aboard a whaler, and we hadn't nothing else to fuck; so I used to fuck the cook up the ass!'

His partner, of course, did not understand a word that he said. She looks at him inquiringly, and says, 'Oh Shiete,' meaning, 'Teach me.'

The girl repeats the word, and works his prick furiously. She is a practised hand at it.

'Oh! My! Oh! My! Oh! My! – Look out, Betsy, I am going to squirt!'

I paid no further attention; for, to tell the truth, I was in the same boat. The most delightful sensations came over me. I plied my finger quickly in and out of her slit. Then I took her up in my arms and kissed it a dozen times. But she was hot with lust, and was at my prick again in a moment. She worked it fiercely. I sucked her lips with mine. Then she placed both hands on my tool.

I felt her spending.

'I cannot last much longer,' I cried. 'Not a minute.'

With that I threw a silken covering over my penis and squirted into it a number of times. Then I lay back and gasped with satisfaction.

I fairly pawed her cunt, and pinched and cuddled it in various ways; and meanwhile she was still at my prick like a milkmaid at a cow's teat. I was conscious of nothing else.

The faint sound of a gong was heard as in a dream. In an instant the maids disappeared; and then for some time, nothing was heard from anyone but sighs of pleasure.

The old Ned was the first to speak.

'That was a jerk-off dessert,' he observes. 'Oh! Be God! But it was fine! Them ere girls know how to jerk – eh, Daimy?'

Saigo now speaks.

'The charming maidens who have just left are the most expert in their line in all Japan. They are employed by the nobility and the wealthy classes, and are known as Yu-Shoku-Nesans (late dinner waitresses). They are virgins. When their virginity is lost, they turn Geishas.'

We all felt fine, for every one of us had been jerked off by the artistic maidens in the most superb manner.

'So jerking off is a fine art in Japan. I never knew the capabilities of the art before,' says the Lieutenant Harris.

'Yes,' chimes in the old Ned. 'It was just great! Why, that ere little devil stretched me prick so that it looks young again. I was just agoin' to stick it in her quim when off she goes. – Say, Daimy, ask the boss if he can't give us something to fuck.'

'Be silent, fool!' commanded the Lieutenant Harris in a severe tone.

We were all still enjoying the sensations caused by the girl's handlings. Some had one leg negligently placed over the other. Saigo reclined at full length. The merchant, who had enjoyed the jerk – off for a longer period than the rest, was now slowing spending.

Champagne was passed around freely.

'Save your stomachs,' said our host, in warning. 'Remember, the orgy has just begun.'

The soft sound of the gong is again heard. The hangings rattle like hail, and a beautiful young girl enters. She throws open her kimono and then dances like a fairy. Then the robe falls to the floor, and we behold her entirely naked.

She is a glorious specimen of ripening womanhood. Her bosom is round and full. Her arms are absolutely perfect. Dimples display themselves at the elbow. But oh! Ye Gods! What a slit! It distracts me to gaze at it. As she dances, one leg is thrown up, and she spins on the other, thus affording us a fine view of all her beauties.

Expressions of admiration come from all.

'That cunt would change an Empire!' cries Itsogoyu.

'Look at the dimpled thing!' exclaims the Lieutenant Harris. 'What a treasure!'

'Good God! How I would like to open those close lips!' says the Ensign Budd.

'Jumpin' Moses!' shouts the old Ned. 'That cunt takes the biscuit! – Oh! Where did you get it? – Come, girlee!' he shouts, beckoning to her. 'Look at this nice prick! It's a regular liver-tickler.'

The dancer is heedless of the summons. She next wields a

huge fan which covers her front completely. Then she turns and gives us a fine back view. Her arse is perfect. Quick as a flash, she reverses. Then she throws herself upon a divan and reproduces the motions of the sexual combat. This is done in such admirable style that we all instantly start forward.

As for me, the performance I have just described makes me nearly furious with sexual excitement. I start forward, and begin to perform an outlandish dance. I push the old Ned down on the floor and stand on him.

'Bring me a cunt!' I shout. 'My prick is bursting!'

'Get off me back!' he cries. 'I ain't got no cunt – Watch him masters, or he'll plug me asshole up!'

I spurn the prostrate form with my foot.

'Dog!' I reply, losing command of myself.

'Japanese gentlemen never fuck arse-holes. They fuck cunt – Do you hear me? C-U-N-T!'

As I speak these words, the gong again sounds, and six entirely nude females enter.

'Ha!' whispers Itsogoyu. 'They are all members of the ballet at Hanami-Kogi. God of Gods. He must have paid an immense sum to bring them here!'

Saigo now speaks.

'Restrain yourself a moment, most noble Daimio. First join in the dance with these fair dames.'

Saying this, he throws off his covering, and in a trice is stark naked. We all follow his example. Invisible music is heard. Each man takes a partner, and the revel begins.

I secure a perfect Venus. She is not more than twenty, yet she is as luscious as a ripe peach. Her plump fair bosom is a feast in itself. Her shapely limbs are without a flaw. The dark, flushing, crimson-tinted cheeks and scarlet lips are enchanting to behold.

'By Jizo! You angel!' I shout, 'I could eat you! – Oh! Great God! Look at this prick! – Let me toy with your slit. Ha! Ha! 'Tis moist! – How often do you fuck, girl? – Now feel my prick. Have you ever before handled such a fine one?'

My words are cut short by a stinging slap on the arse.

'Wake up, Daimy, old boy. Get out of me road!' I hear the old Ned say. 'Oh I've got a snorter! – Jesus! I just kissed her cunt! Now I'll kiss her ass! Then I'll fuck her like hell! – All right, Lieutenant, – I'll get out of the way. – Come Susie! – To hell with dancing! I want to get me prick into this! – Oh! But ain't it nice! – Jump, you devil! Jump! Wait til I put the other finger in your quim! Ha! I thought that would wake you up! – Now lay down there! That's good! – Ah! That's damn good!'

Meanwhile the rest are dancing about with great fervour. The Lieutenant Harris's partner has hold of his prick. He has a hand between her thighs. They both enjoy it immensely.

The merchant has already stuck his fine tool into his graceful partner's slit, and thus joined they dance and gyrate about. Not far from them the Ensign Budd's partner is dancing violently about him, alternately pulling his tool and kissing it.

Our host, Saigo, is down on his knees before a glorious slit which is hovering constantly about him. She is teasing his prick into an iron rigidity which she will presently enjoy to the full.

I see all this when fingering my partner.

'Master! Master!' she protests. 'Do you not feel me coming? Why do you tantalize me thus?'

'Darling one,' I cry, withdrawing my fingers and greedily kissing her lovely slit. 'Pardon me! I will not make you wait a second longer.'

Saying this I push open the lips of her treasure spot with my eager prick, and work my arse strongly until I am in to the balls.

The pleasure sets me wild. I shout. I dance. I sing. The rest of the company likewise are heard. They are all, like myself, out of their senses, and fuck the women like madmen. Never before or since have I seen such a fucking match.

The old Ned's voice is heard above the rest.

'This is rich, this is! – Oh! Jesus! How – I – would – like – to keep – this up – for a week! – But I am agoin' to come! – Whoop! Whoop! There it goes! – Jumpin' Jesus! This takes the biscuit.'

Nor can I hold in much longer. One more round, and then I fall back on the couch. But the Kuge will not have it so.

'Make your way to your apartments!' he cries.

We all obey. There we fuck until we are tired out, and fall asleep in each other's arms.

Most courteous reader, I would recount to you further details were it in my power.

Alas! I have received notice that my narration is becoming of an undue length. Perhaps at some later period we may meet again.

A few days after the events just related, the most noble Americans departed for Yokohama to rejoin their ship. Our parting was indeed sorrowful. My affection for them was beyond my power of expression. Before leaving I gave to the Lieutenant Harris the copies of the astronomical observations I had promised him. The Ensign Budd, wishing to leave me a souvenir, presented me his diary, some pages of which form the introduction to my narrative. I shall cherish them always for the sake of their former owner.

Honourable reader, the Daimio of Satsuma thus salutes you. I thank you for your kind attention. Should it ever be your fortune to visit my beloved Japan, may the pleasure of meeting you be mine. And now I bid you a last farewell. I wish you good luck in all your amours, and I pray that Amida will always grant you, in the supreme moment of love's most ecstatic bliss, a stiffness in your sexual parts that will rival that of our esteemed and noble friend, Itsogoyu.

Blind Lust

PART I

I have often been asked to write my memoirs. I have always resisted the blandishments of mere curiosity, however I will yield to yours, my dear Lucien, for I firmly believe in the sincerity of the affection which bound us together during so many years despite the combined witchcrafts of time and absence.

Besides has not my sweetest law always been to obey your will?

Not so, I hear you murmur. I assure you that I am telling you the plain truth, and to punish you for your wicked doubt, I will compel you to follow me into the country, far enough removed from the place in which we actually dwell.

It is towards the Garden of France that we must turn our steps; at some kilometres from Tours, a pleasant city near which lies the Chateau de Pauvanne, the abode of the Marquis de Pauvanne, my grandmother.

It was within the walls of this handsome thirteenth century edifice that the days of my infancy and my youth slipped by.

Sequestered beneath the shade of the venerable trees, adorned with magnificent flowers, refreshed by a dainty stream with its capricious meanderings bathing the skirt of the park, it offered to the glance the most picturesque aspect that one could dream of.

Like the greater part of the young girls belonging to the local aristocracy, my studies took place at the Convent de Marmouniers.

Then as I grew up, my grandmother desirous of seeing my youth make sunny her white hairs, came one day and took me from the arms of Mother Eudoxie, and carried me off to Pauvanne.

From the child which I had been the day before, I now became a young lady; I had my suite of rooms and my own waiting maid and this seemed to me to be infinitely more delightful than my residence at Marmoutiers.

Not, however, that my life was gay at Pauvanne, no, my grandmother was no longer able to go about; her legs scarcely permitting her to walk even a short distance in the grounds. Hence being unable to accompany her, she gave me full liberty to come and go within the walled enclosures of Pauvanne.

The estate being of considerable extent, I had plenty of elbow room, and I profitted by it to explore it to the utmost recesses.

My greatest happiness was to wander in its wildest nooks, and even to lose myself therein, in the reveries of a girl of seventeen.

These reveries were, I ought to own, always of the same nature.

A strange vagueness pervaded my soul; my imagination flew off to unknown regions, and presented to my eyes images of tenderness and devotion in which a young and beautiful man always became the hero.

Although profoundly ignorant with regard to the difference of sex, my senses, already awakened, stirred throughout my entire organism. Flashes of scorching blood often obscured my sight, my legs trembled and I was obliged to sit down, compelled by the influence of an enervating sensation at once painful and pleasing.

I had left the convent at Easter, and April and May intoxicated me with their odours of springtime; and June despite the heat, could only increase my desire for these solitary strolls.

It was in the morning, beyond all other times, that I made my escape, not yet having lost the habit of early rising which the Nuns inculcate in their pupils. And I have often seen the first rays of the sun issue from the midst of the night and make golden the heaths and fir plantations of Pauvanne.

On my return from one of these excursions, I heard my grandmother announce the expected arrival of my aunt, Helene, news which caused me to cry out in joy.

Helene de Torcol was twenty-five years old and ravishingly beautiful. For the past two years she had been the widow of the Baron de Torcol, an old man of eighty, with whom her twenty years of age had been cynically associated.

Happily, the Baron promptly took the step of departing to the Lord to ask him for the recompense of his merits and his widow found herself free, without children, and with a yearly income of two hundred thousand francs.

She was certainly the most ravishing person that one could dream of. Her hair, black as ebony, set off the whiteness of her complexion and it was lit up by the radiancy of the two large brown eyes. Her wide and sensual mouth was habitually slightly open revealing her pearly pointed teeth. Imperceptible black down slightly marked her upper lips and revealed a nature by no means destitute of virility.

Neither too tall nor too short, her dainty figure admirably shaped, with the hand and feet of a child, she appeared to me and to many others of marvellous beauty.

I adored her, her lively vivacious character had long before captivated me, and then accustomed to living in the company of an old lady, I always regarded the coming of Helene as the signal for a crowd of distractions.

We had passed a year together at Marmoutiers, where she was in the highest and I in the lowest class, so I looked upon her more as a friend than as a relation.

For some months back there had been talk of her proposed marriage to the Count de Vycabre, and my grandmother who approved the match, had written to the Count inviting him to pay a visit to the Chateau.

The Count did not need pressing and a few days later came and installed himself at Pauvanne.

The proximity, so close to me, of this engaged couple brought a notable perturbation into my life.

Here we touch upon a delicate matter and I do not know in truth that I can talk about it chastely.

Let Dame Chastity sleep! I hear you insinuate to me.

Alas! I greatly fear that in effect, it will have to be so, and arming myself with an imperturbable assurance I continue.

One morning very early in accordance with my custom, I had hidden myself deep in the park. Seated at the foot of a tree, my mind plunged in vague reverie, I lost all count of time, when an unexpected noise called my to my senses, and I heard steps coming in my direction.

Much perplexed I sank down and, putting aside the foliage, I perceived the profile of my aunt, who was clothed in white and blue morning gown.

M. de Vycabre in a Nanking undress, with a straw hat on his head accompanied her.

They seemed to be talking very eagerly and instinct warned me to avoid their seeing me. I concealed myself behind a dense clump of trees.

The promenaders soon stood still near me, M. de Vycabre glanced round him and his inspection doubtless convinced him that no one could observe them, for he threw his arms around my aunt's waist and drawing her to him, pressed her against his breast. Their lips met and I heard the exchange of a long kiss.

Without understanding the reason, I felt my heart beating violently as I overheard these words –

'I love you passionately. What a frightful time I have passed without you, my angel – my sweet beloved one – my dear Helene, we shall never leave each other again. Come closer so that I can again be kissed by your lovely eyes, your pretty teeth, your delicious neck – ah, I could eat you!'

My aunt, far from resisting, abandoned herself to him and returned kiss for kiss and caress for caress; her colour was heightened and her beautiful eyes were half closed.

'My Rene!' she said, 'I love you as much as you love me, I belong to you entirely!'

The sight of these caresses produced an indescribable effect in me. My senses quickened as though struck by an electric spark and I almost lost consciousness.

However, I at once regained my self possession and continued to be all eyes and ears.

M. Rene was asking for something which I did not understand, and he appeared to be pressing his request.

'No,' replied Helene, 'not here, I beg of you, I should never dare. Mon Dieu! if anybody were to see us, I should die of it.'

'But dearest, how can anybody see us at this hour?'

'I don't know, but I am afraid. Stay – do you see I could have no pleasure; we will seek a means to come together, I pray you.'

'How can you talk to me of patience in the state I am in? Give me your little hand, judge for yourself.'

The Count took my aunt's hand and put it squarely between his legs so that it was impossible for me to explain to myself the motive. My astonishment became much greater when I saw her hand quickly disappear in a gap that she had quickly unbuttoned.

What she found there I was unable to judge, I saw nothing, but I heard her say with the tenderest inflection:

'Dear Mimi, I see that you have a great desire! And how beautiful you are, I also wish for it greatly, if we only had some shelter I could so quickly put you to right!'

And her little hand moved itself sweetly up and down, while M. de Vycabre stood motionless and enrapt, his legs slightly apart and seemed to enjoy a lively pleasure. After a moment's silence, my aunt exclaimed:

'Ah!' – then suddenly – 'what an idea! Come, I recollect there is a convenient pavilion near by, you understand me – it is a singular place in which to screen our love, but no one will see us and I can be entirely yours – come!'

The pavilion of which my aunt spoke had been constructed with a foresight of the feebleness of poor humanity and was in the shape of a cottage of two rooms, it was in good order, so that in case of being surprised by a heavy shower, one might take refuge there.

Protected as I was by the high shrubbery, I could approach the place without fear of being seen. I managed this with infinite precautions and arrived behind the pavilion just as Helene and M. de Vycabre entered.

The Count after casting a glance around the grounds to see if they had been watched, shut the door and pushed the bolt on the inside which protected the entrance of this convenient hidey-hole. I looked about for a commodious observatory and it was speedily found.

The boards and tree trunk, badly joined, presented me with a sufficient opening to see plainly. I placed my eyes to it and held my breath, being witness to that which I shall now describe.

Helene hanging on the neck of M. de Vycabre, devoured him with kisses.

'Come, my dear,' she said, 'it was with a very bad grace that I refused you, but fear prevented me. Here at least I feel reassured. And this good Mimi, what a feast I am going to give him! Stay, thinking about it is nothing, how shall we fix ourselves?'

The pavilion was furnished very primitively, in the first apartment was a wooden seat with a large tree trunk and its branches for a back.

'Rest quietly, we will find a suitable position, but first let me look at Biby – it is so long since I examined her that I am convulsed with desire.'

I delivered myself up to strange reflections on hearing this dialogue and on seeing their actions. What were they going to do? I was not long in finding out.

M. de Vycabre going on one knee, lifted up Helene's petticoats and chemise and seemed to fall into ecstasy.

Under a delicate cambric chemise were revealed two legs worthy of Venus and perfectly moulded, clad in silk stockings, fastened above the knee with flame-coloured garters.

Then above these garters, two adorable thighs, white round and firm which joined one another at their sumit, under a fleece of black and lustrous hair, the abundance of which astonished me; for whilst watching I thought of the slight nut brown moss which was beginning to show on me and cover the same parts of my body.

'How I love it,' said the Count, 'how beautiful and fresh it is, my pretty Biby – dearest, open your tiny legs a little so that I may kiss it!'

Helene did as she was asked, her thighs unclosed themselves and allowed me to see the little rosy cleft to which her lover glued his lips.

Helene seemed to be transported, she closed her eyes, incoherent words escaped from her throat, whilst she lent herself to this strange caress by a slight movement.

'Ah, I am dying!' she cried after a moment, 'ah!'

'What is it then, Bon Dieu?' I asked myself, the thought of a caress on this part of the body never having come to me before. I could not see how any one could get pleasure by it, yet I began to feel in the same part ticklings that were of an enlightening nature.

M. de Vycabre raised himself and supported my aunt, whose enervation seemed to be so excessive. This state of prostration did not last long. Helene soon recovered her senses and, entwining her arms around his neck, she kissed him ardently.

'Come my adored one,' she said, 'but how?'

'Turn around, dearest, and lean on this clumsy bit of furniture.'

To my great stupefaction Helene stood up and with rapid and feverish movements undid the Count's trousers and tucked his shirt up under his waistcoat. Then I saw an object so extraordinary to me that I was on the point of crying out.

What could this unknown member be, the rosy head and length and thickness of which seemed so monstrous to me?

Helene did not seem to share my fears, for she took it in her hand, the unknown which had caused my fright – caressed it for a few minutes and said:

'Come, Monsieur Mimi, come to your little friend, and above all, don't come too quickly!'

On saying which my aunt drew up her dress from behind and displayed to the Counts and to me, two little rondures of a dazzling whiteness divided by a line of which I saw but a faint trace.

Then, bending down and placing her hands on the rustic wooden bench, she presented her lover with an elegant croup.

Rene, standing behind her, took in his hand this I-knew-not-what which had so astonished me and commenced to introduce it between the lips which I perceived.

Helene did not stir, she opened as wide as possible the part which jutted out so. Little by little, I saw this dilate and as speedily absorb the monstrosity. The operation was so complete that the stomach of M. de Vycabre was glued against my aunt's buttocks.

Then there took place between them a come and go of combined movements, incoherent talk and broken words.

'Ah, how I love you! You are penetrating me,' said Helene, 'ah, my love, go softly – leave me alone for a moment, ah-ha – more quickly, now – now – I'm dying – ah, ah!'

I looked at Rene, his eyes were half closed, his hands resting on my aunt's hips, he seemed to be in a state of inexpressible beatitude.

'Stay, my angel, – my all!' he said, 'ah, how good it is to be happy, you are happy – is it not so? I feel you are with me – enjoy well my dearest!'

Both rested for a few minutes. My aunt as though swooning, did not change her position, at last she turned her head slightly and giving her lover a kiss, said to him:

'Now together, you will let me know when you are ready.'

Their motion recommenced. At the end of a few moments, the Count in his turn exclaimed:

'Ah, dearest are you . . . – I can wait no longer!'

'Yes – yes – go – I follow you! I . . .'

Her voice trailed off into silence while M. de Vycabre seemed almost to give way in his turn and fall on my aunt, who had to rest firmly on her wrists in order to resist his weight.

Then he drew back a little and I saw his astonishing instrument again as it withdrew from the retreat in which it had been so well cased and feasted. But how changed it seemed to me – half as large and reddened. In fact it was no longer the same at all.

The Count put his clothes straight, whilst my aunt raised herself and, throwing her arms round her companion's neck, kissed him tenderly. A calm took possession of them, but not of me. The warm breezes of the fir tree forest blew against me in vain and the morning songs of the birds did not distract me in the least.

My brain whirled – my imagination heated to the utmost degree, caused me to feel a portion of the pleasures of which I had been a witness. I drew up my petticoats, my chemise, and with an inexperienced hand I commenced to explore this tender part, thus assuring myself that I was made like Helene, but without knowing yet what relief this hand of mine could procure me.

I was soon to find out.

After many kisses Helene said to the Count:

'Listen, my dear, I have thought about it – you know that my rooms are situated in the Chateau quite by themselves. My waiting maid is away, no one could dream of our rendezvous, and we could pass some adorable nights together.

'I will send Marcelle to Paris at once under some pretext or other and every evening shall reunite us; so be on the look out, a sign will warn you during the day as to the hour at which it will be safe to slip into my room.

'I trust you to take the most minute precautions.'

It was then decided that M. de Vycabre should leave the little hut first and take a stroll through the park in order to give my aunt a chance to regain her chamber by the servant's staircase.

The Count disappeared and I remained squatted amongst my shrubbery until he was out of sight.

As Madame de Torcol did not at once make her appearance I once more glanced within.

This dainty retreat amidst the trees was furnished with a wash stand and a jug of water in a serviceable condition.

I saw Helene fill the hand basin, raise her petticoats and stand over it. In the position I occupied, I could see her pretty little cleft open itself. It seemed to me to be of vivid carnation but the sides, the interior and even as far as the thick underwood which surrounded it, seemed to have been plunged into a kind of glutinous fluid.

Helene began an ample ablution and I was preparing to steal gently away when one of her movements stupefied me.

At the commencement of the operation, my aunt's hand carefully refreshed the fatigued parts, but all at once she stopped. Her finger placed itself on a slight eminence situated right in front of where she began to rub, at first lightly and slowly, then with a kind of fury. At last she seemed to experience the pleasurable sensations of the minute before.

I had seen enough – I understood and was not long in vanishing – a winding alley conducted me to the Chateau where, my brain on fire, my bosom palpitating and with a staggering gait, I re-entered my chamber with the firm intention of enjoying on my own accounts, the last act of the pantomime that I had witnessed.

That wherein no partner was required.

Like one demented, I flung my hat on the floor, then shut and double-locked the door, threw myself on the bed, flung my clothes up to the waist and struggled to use my hand in the way that I had seen Helene use hers to gain satisfaction.

Several attempts proved ineffectual but at last, with Nature helping me, the sensitive point revealed itself and the remainder became easy, for my observation had been through.

A delicious sensation seized me, I continued furiously and speedily, and the ecstasy experienced became such that I actually lost consciousness. When I returned to myself I found that I was still in the same position, my hand was all wet with an unknown dew and it was not for a considerable time that I was able to completely recover my senses.

Breakfast time was at hand, I made a hasty toilette and went down stairs.

My aunt, stretched out in an easy chair, was chatting with my grandmother, beautiful and fresh and unflushed, as though she had just arisen from an excellent night's rest.

I had need to assure myself that I had not dreamt it all and that Helene had, like all virtuous folk seen the sun rise in her own private bedroom, rather than as I knew, elsewhere.

As for myself, I felt that I looked ugly, my eyes were discoloured, my cheeks were flushed and even grandmother noticed my agitation. I assured her that I felt perfectly well and my aunt kissed me and we began to talk about different subjects. When M. de Vycabre entered the room all my self-possession had returned to me.

In the most natural manner he related to us how he had

made an excursion to a neighbouring village, and we sat down to the table.

Without appearing to do so, I did not let a single gesture from my aunt or the Count escape me, but I was disappointed because not a sign or a look disclosed their plan to me.

During dessert, my aunt said carelessly to my grandmother, 'I was so thoughtless on leaving Paris, that I shall be obliged to send my maid to fetch me a lot of things.'

'Oh, Mon Dieu, who will take her place here with you?'

'Don't trouble yourself about that, I can attend to myself perfectly well during so short an absence.'

The day passed without incident, M. de Vycabre mounted his horse and took a long ride, while we sat by the side of the lake and did some needlework.

Some neighbours called on us and grandmother kept them to dinner and in the evenings we had some music. M. de Vycabre devoted himself to whist with Madame de Pauvanne and was perfectly reserved towards us.

I hastened to find myself alone, face to face with my thoughts.

Immediately eleven o'clock struck I went to bed, quickly dismissing my maid, not doubting but that tomorrow night a serious rendezvous would take place between M. de Vycabre and my aunt, so I ran over the means at my disposal of spying on the impassioned scenes which I was sure would be the consequence.

Knowing every nook and corner of the house, I began at once to draw up a plan of campaign, of which the small suite of apartments occupied by my aunt, became the centre of operations.

We both lodged in the middle story of the Chateau, but at the opposite extremities of the same corridor. All the rooms on this story opened on the same corridor. M. de Vycabre was also lodged on this floor but in an angular wing.

My aunt's suite consisted of a bedroom, drawing-room and a little room in which was fixed a bed for her waiting maid.

I recalled to mind a certain dressing-room occupying only a third of the length of the room, which had formerly led to an alcove but had afterwards been closed up by a strong partition wall.

A bull's eye window let in at the top of the alcove had been merely stopped up by a pierglass representing a pastoral scene, (in truth a bad enough oil painting). I equally well remembered a kind of black cabinet and my plan was complete. I went to sleep full of resolution and hope for the coming day.

Marcelle set off the next morning as arranged.

M. de Vycabre and my aunt were more than ever reserved, however I was able to catch what I wanted to know – the hour of the rendezvous.

After breakfast the Count leaned nonchalantly against the mantelpiece and, while admiring a handsome clock, a superb ball-shaped article, he let his finger rest for a moment on the figures XI and VI – I easily translated this mute language, half past eleven and when my aunt replied with a slight motion of her eyes, I was certain.

We went to sit in the garden and M. de Vycabre who contrary to his custom had remained at home, started to read to us. I then escaped on some pretext and went up to the second floor.

There I drew a table to the door, placed a stool upon it and, without pity for the artist's work, cut a hole in the pastoral scene and proved to myself that I could occupy a front box to see what was going to take place in my aunt's room. Finally, satisfied with my invention, I returned to the others.

Time seemed to me to drag its moments out to a mortal length.

At last half-past ten struck, my grandmother retired and we followed her example.

M. de Vycabre wished us good night and went to his room; my aunt stopped with me for a few minutes longer and then conducted me to my chamber where she left me after kissing me tenderly.

I was not slow in undressing that night, you may be sure; and my maid remarked that I must be in need of sleep to make such haste.

This was not altogether the motive which made me hasten the departure of my maid, for scarcely was she out of my room when I again put on my stockings and slippers and a dark-coloured wrapper and waited.

At about a quarter past eleven I glided towards my scaffolding; scrambled up to the top and installed myself as comfortably as I could, then gazed as though I was at a theatre.

I saw very distinctly the white and fresh-looking bed resembling an altar prepared for the sacrifice; a lamp on the table flooded it with vivid light.

Helene was in her dressing room where I heard her making ablutions of various kinds; for I heard the sound of a certain instrument which I was sure she was putting up herself.

Her operations concluded, I saw her come into the room clad only in a dressing gown; she went to the bed and turned down the clothes, arranged the pillows and, moved the lamp so that it more nearly faced it.

Divesting herself of her wrapper, she undid the fine

cambric chemise that still concealed her form and stepped up to the mirror. She admired herself for a second, before letting the chemise drop with a gracious movement of her shoulders till it rested on her haunches and slipped to the floor. Then Helene, the pretty Helene, appeared completely naked to my dazzled eyes.

One couldn't dream of anything more beautiful, – her breasts were firm and high, round and luscious, tipped by two nipples of a vivid rose while the dimpled curve of her hips and buttocks was mouth-watering even to an admirer of her own sex.

The base of her stomach, white and polished as ivory, displayed her conspicuously luxurious ebony fleece, of which the length and density made a rare sight. The contrast between this black triangle and her lush white flesh gave Helene a particular stamp of lascivious strangeness.

The charming woman again drew on her chemise and replaced her dressing gown, tying the girdle negligently, then going to the door of her room left it slightly ajar.

A moment afterward, with a thousand precautions, M. de Vycabre entered and carefully locked the door behind him.

The Count, his bare feet in slippers, was attired in a summer morning gown, beneath which I could see he wore only his shirt.

Helene made him sit down on a sofa and perched herself on his knee and their mouths met in a long kiss, while they spoke of their marriage. An obstacle, not yet surmounted, delayed the event but, according to the Count, matters would be speedily concluded.

'Dear angel,' he said, 'you will never sufficiently know how grateful I am to you for having had confidence in me and not making me wait for my possession of you. I adore you, my dear Helene and I shall always do so, always – do you hear?'

While he was saying this, the Count was opening the neck of my aunt's wrapper and began kissing her breasts with frenzy.

My aunt, her head thrown back, quivered under his caress and, a voluptuous shudder agitated her.

Rene, profiting by this movement, opened her wrapper still further but this time at the bottom and, raising her chemise, he played for a moment with her beautiful black fleece, which he seemed to delight in. It was the imitation of this activity had given me so much pleasure the day before.

Helene on her side, brought to light the beautiful member on which my eyes became fixed – it appeared to me to be even larger and longer than the last time. My aunt stretched apart her thighs, opening by this movement her little cleft, which did not seem to be longer than my little finger.

'How,' said I to myself, 'could it be possible for an instrument of these dimensions to penetrate entirely into so small a space?'

I came to the conclusion that the first time I had observed my aunt, she had doubtless not taken the huge machine actually inside her but placed it between her thighs; and that it was her rubbing it there that had made him so happy. My error was to be of short duration.

During my reflections the two lovers had continued giving each other the sweet caresses I have mentioned.

'Ah,' said Helene, 'my dear little husband, go on – ah, I am happy. How beautiful Mimi is – how I am going to enjoy it – it is coming – eh – oh – do it a little more, I am dying.'

A little moment of silence – Helene lay prostrate her body thrown backwards, her head hidden in her lover's shoulders, her thighs apart, she lay as though in a swoon, and M. de Vycabre contemplated her with delight.

'Come now,' said Helene, recovering and suddenly raising herself ' – come and put it into me – I want to feel it entirely – come I am on fire – I burn; come Monsieur Mimi, come and sprinkle me with your good liquor.'

Helene untied her wrapper, threw it on the floor, as she did her chemise, then stretched herself on the bed; Rene did the same with his morning gown and, before placing himself on Helene, he raised his shirt clear up to his armpits. He was truly beautiful and his naked body brought to my mind both Hercules and Apollo. His nude torso straightened itself in all its splendour. His fiery instrument stood out boldly from a thick underwood which set if off. He then got upon the bed.

Helene had remained in the same position, with her legs a little apart and bent upwards. Rene was now able to look her all over. I waited to see her raise herself and turn her behind to her lover like the first time, for I believed that it could not be done otherwise. But to my great astonishment this proved not to be the case.

M. de Vycabre knelt over her. Helene raised her legs and placed them across his loins in such a manner that nothing could escape my view. So I distinctly saw Helene's hand seize his instrument and direct its head to the centre of her little gap, which seemed to partly open to receive it.

M. de Vycabre gave a vigorous thrust of the loins, Helene responded with a similar one, and at least half of his machine penetrated into that hungry little mouth, which stretched itself to swallow accommodate its prize. Several successive movement finished the introduction and I saw their two fleeces mingle greedily.

This time I knew what to believe. There was now nothing

more than a union of movements, sighs, inarticulate words, quiverings as if they had become lunatics.

'Give it all to me,' said Helene. 'Ah, how good it is, move softly – we will enjoy a long time.'

'Dearest, move and raise your thighs a little more so that I can enter better, now do you feel it? Ah, what delight! I am dying!'

'Are you ready, my Rene – as for me – I – I – hurry yourself!'

'I am – there it is coming – it is rising – now – I come, I am doing it! Oh, ah! I am coming!'

Both remained motionless for a moment, then Rene raised himself and I saw his dear instrument come out like the first time, red and tear-stained.

Helene remained a long time without giving a sign of life then, raising herself, she covered Rene with kisses and passed for an instant into her dressing room.

I believed everything to be finished and thought of retiring, but a secret presentment made me remain.

Helene returned and lay down again, put her arms round her lover and a sweet conversation took place between them.

'My friend, how happy I have been! How much better it is when one is quite relaxed. How well you know how to give pleasure.'

'Dearest, there doesn't exist in the whole world a more perfect woman than yourself, and I want to eat you all up!' And, again lifting up Helene's chemise, Rene covered her lovely body with kisses. Arriving at the very centre of pleasure, he half opened it, bit it sweetly and kissed it passionately.

'Stop, my friend,' said Helene,' 'stop, you will fatigue yourself!'

'No, dearest, look – see, it again asks permission to come to its little companion.'

'Let us see, Monsieur Mimi – what! already returned to this fine state? You are very beautiful and I love you. Come, I am weak, I spoil you, come and imprison yourself once more there, there, place yourself like that and don't budge!'

'What are you going to do?'

'You know, my friend, that I love a change! Stay on your back and I will be the one who is to do it.'

While saying this, my aunt straddled Rene, and taking M. Mimi in her hand, she buried it in her up to the hilt; then, regulating her movements, she squatted down on his body and remained there impaled by his enormous pivot. She incited Rene, brought kisses to him, showed him her adorable titties, while all the while making faces at him.

'I am playing your part,' she said, 'you are my little wife – see how well I do it.'

It was soon easy to see that the critical moment had arrived; the young woman lay over her lover, who received her in his arms, and pressed her onto him by holding her white buttocks with both hands.

The pleasure seized them again both together, then Helene disengaged herself softly and again lay by her lover's side.

It was late and I was overwhelmed with emotion and fatigue. The position I occupied was not comfortable but I did not wish to depart before discovering whether the amorous couple would make another rendezvous.

My patience was rewarded as I heard them fix the same hour for the next night.

I then regained my room and went to bed exhausted. Sleep came promptly to me, and I woke at seven o'clock the next morning, perfectly rested. Then I went over in my mind what I had heard and seen the night before.

At once my imagination became inflamed, my breast heaved and fire coursed through my veins. I lay on my back in the position my aunt had taken, then I raised my chemise the way M. de Vycabre had done.

I fondled my breasts, whose buds had scarcely formed, and felt them swell gently then, caressing my body, I arrived at the delicate part which fascinated me the most.

It seemed to me that a slight change had taken place there. I found the lips of this little retreat plumper, I felt the passage which – in my aunt's case – had swallowed up the enormous machine, and to my surprise I found only a little hole which my finger could not penetrate without pain. Then I moved my finger a little higher and an indescribable sensation invaded my whole being. I rubbed softly at first, then more quickly, then slackened, then hastened, all the while repeating my aunt's words:

'Ah, how good it is – I am going in, ah!' At last a nervous spasm seized me and I was transported on a flood of immense happiness and all the feelings remained with me, for I did not lose consciousness as I had the other time.

When I had quite recovered, I withdrew my moist hand, then got up and dressed myself, and went downstairs fresh and happy.

I will not relate the day's doings, which contained nothing of interest. I was careful, however, to be present at the evening rendezvous, and had arrived without accident at my observatory when Helene and her lover met again.

The preliminaries were similar to those of the night before, but instead of afterwards retiring to bed, Helene said:

'My friend, I have a caprice, let us do it like we did the

other morning in the pavilion. We are so much more comfortable and it will be so much nicer!'

While saying this, she took off her peignoir, drew her chemise up from behind, placed her hands on a great cushion near the glazed wardrobe and fixed herself there. In this position her head and arms were lower than her buttocks which lifted up and defined by this ravishing pose, plainly presented a heavenly path to pleasure.

Rene, too, made his preparations. He took off his dressing gown and placed the lamp on the floor in such a way as to perfectly delicious tableau – which was also reflected in the mirrored wardrobe. Then he set himself to work.

'Ah, you see too much!' said my aunt.

'Could I see too much of so many beauties – look in the glass.'

'Ah, no, it is too much! Ah, oh, stop a little – oh, how beautiful you are thus.'

'My adored one, how lovely you are – what admirable haunches – what an adorable arse you have.'

'Ah, Rene, what a villainous word that is.'

'Don't be frightened, dearest, everything is permitted in love; these words, so out of place elsewhere, give piquancy to its sweet mysteries. You will also say them and then you will understand their charm.'

All the time he was speaking, he continued his motions. Helene held still and spoke no word, but devoured the glass with her eyes. I was stupified to hear her say a moment afterwards:

'You love it well then?'

'What?'

'Well, eh, my . . .'

'Your what?'

'Well, my . . . arse . . .'

'Oh, Helene, how bonny you are! Oh, yes, I love it. I adore your beautiful bottom, I adore it!'

'Well, caress it then; it is all yours – my bot – bot-bottom.'

In finishing these broken words she let herself go in complete enjoyment; Rene who had also arrived at the sovereign pleasure, clasped her tightly and almost swooned on her.

In this way they terminated the evening with this delicious caresses; they could not make another rendezvous, fearing the waiting maid's return from Paris, but agreed on certain signals. If the worst came to the worst, they could meet at the pavilion in the park.

I regained my room, Marcelle returned the next day and the nocturnal meetings could no longer be held. I applied myself to interpreting every signal which could be exchanged between the lovers, but was disappointed, as I could discover nothing.

Four days passed thus, I was in despair, continually directing my steps towards the pavilion, only to find it empty.

On the afternoon of the fourth day, having entered the pavilion to satisfy a slight need, I was surprised to see there a garden chair that had evidently been brought from the house. I rightly concluded that the next day would see some activity, so I was there in good time before the actors could take their places.

They came as before, one after the other, with the usual precautions, and carefully fastened themselves in. Helene at once seated herself in the chair and said:

'Truly, you did well to think of this article, for my position the other day was not comfortable. But what are you doing down on your knees?'

'You know very well that I must say good morning to my little companion.'

'Well, give it a kiss quickly and let us hurry – it is late. Seat yourself on the chair and I will get astride you.'

Instantly M. de Vycabre let down his trousers and seated himself on the chair; Helene lifted up her skirts, placed her legs astride her lover, then seized his instrument and slowly introduced it into her channel of love as she lowered her buttocks.

I was placed in the perfect spot to enjoy this spectacle from behind and consequently did not lose a single detail. Very soon the enormous tool completely disappeared inside Helene.

Now she raised her legs, placed her heels on the bars of the chair and began to sink down and rise alternately.

The sighs and familiar words of love came quickly as their spirits dissolved in mutual enjoyment.

I had promised myself that this time I would not simply remain a spectator.

So, at the very moment when Helene introduced M. Mimi, I commenced to caress myself, regulating my movements to theirs, slackening or hastening just as they did. In consequence my sighs arrived so exactly as to be mingled with theirs and were not noticed.

When all was finished, Helene raised herself and quitted her post. As she dismounted, I saw M. Mimi's head emerge from his retreat and with it a sufficiently large amount of liquor to make me wonder. It ran down her thighs to the ground – I was quite unable to account for it! The two lovers then adjusted their clothing.

M. de Vycabre communicated to Helene two letters he had received. The principal obstacle to their marriage had been removed, so it was arranged that in three days M. de Vycabre should make his official request for her hand. Then they agreed to meet in the pavilion two days hence.

I returned to the Chateau very sad; at the prospect of returning to the dull calm of my former life. Happily, the thought that I might soon be married myself sustained my courage, and I certainly promised myself sundry tastes of the illicit pleasures to which I had been a witness.

The next morning but one, I was in my hiding place. M. de Vycabre arrived first, Helene came in a moment later, and I noticed a slight cloud on her beautiful forehead; however, she threw herself into her lover's arms. After some caresses he started to put his hand up under her petticoats, but she stopped him, saying:

'No, my friend, it is impossible today, I am very much grieved, I assure you, but you know – an obstacle – let us wait until they return.'

'Ah, how unhappy I am!'

'And I also.'

'Here, look, how he is longing for it!' And M. de Vycabre drew out of his trousers his resplendant instrument and Helene took it into her hand, saying:

'No, not without me.'

'But I pray you.'

'All right – if you really wish it. One ought not to be selfish; I assure you, it pains me to see such a good thing lost. Come, Monsieur Mimi, but do not accustom yourself to doing it without your companion.'

While speaking, Helene had tucked up the sleeves of her wrapper; M. de Vycabre had dropped his trousers round his feet and raised his shirt out of her way.

'No,' said Helene, 'take off your trousers altogether. Since there is nothing else for me, I want to enjoy all I can with my eyes.'

Rene did as she requested and abandoned himself to her.

She then placed herself just behind him, put her left arm

round his loins, grasped his upstanding limb in her right hand and began to agitate it with a sweet movement of her wrist, alternately covering and uncovering Mimi's head. This activity seemed to procure M. de Vycabre an unheard of degree of pleasure.

'Ah, how well you do it,' said he, 'ah, my angel! Go gently, uncover it well – a little more quickly – now stop, go on again, oh, ah – it is coming, – more quickly yet – I am coming! – I die!'

He gave one or two thrusts of the loins. Helene, who was carefully following his indications, grasped his instrument more tightly in her hand and, to my great astonishment, I saw gush out in jerks of three feet at least, a jet of something white, the emission of which seemed to cause M. de Vycabre delirious happiness.

At the end of several minutes, Helene herself wiped the instrument with her embroidered handkerchief, putting it back in its place and saying:

'You are a wretch, you have enjoyed yourself without me and I am longing for you!'

I let them both retire, and when they were far enough away, I entered the pavilion and closely examined the fresh traces of the ejaculation I had so recently observed.

This sight inflamed my imagination, I threw up my clothes and, getting astride, I placed my hand on the chair, my finger upraised and lowered myself onto it. I found my little opening and, imitating Helene's movements, I began stretching myself to the utmost, raising and lowering my behind. I imagined myself as receiving epic proportions of the real instrument.

A sharp pain did not stop me and I redoubled my efforts till nearly half of my finger entered my grotto.

I then repeated Helene's words: 'I melt! I am doing it!

My arse!'. . . a spasm seized me and I writhed with pleasure.

My hand and the chair both showed marks of my enjoyment and I hastened to erase them before I returned to the Chateau.

During the day, M. de Vycabre had a conference with my grandmother and formally demanded my aunt's hand; they arranged the details and he set off for Paris to rush though the preliminaries.

It was decided that Helene should still remain with us for some days. I was to attend the marriage as her bridesmaid, so she took me away with her.

The wedding was celebrated with great style and for the first time in my life I attended a grand ball, at which, I can say without vanity, I was a veritable success.

I should have dearly loved to witness the bedding of the newly married couple, but unhappily my observatory was not in that house, and I had to resign myself to a solitary association in their pleasures.

Three days later, M. de Vycabre brought me back to my grandmother and set off with his wife to Italy.

After the departure of the newly married couple, I fell back into the monotony of my former existence with my senses wakened and the knowledge of some pleasures that my ardent nature rendered necessary to me.

To me M. de Vycabre had become the beau ideal of a husband.

The pavilion in the park retain some strong memories for me, and I often visited it. I had left the chair there and it served as the throne for my solitary pleasures.

These means of solace were not only necessary but at

times indispensable, for I was often taken with veritable amorous furies, my eyes clouded, my ears rang, my legs faltered under me, and just by closing my thighs one against the other, I agitated that charming spot which makes us women become moist.

In those moments no resistance was possible, I could not help myself. My finger became a past master and, after I had thoroughly pleasured myself, I felt a calm and delicious freshness circulate through me and I am convinced that without this, I should have had some serious illness. Happily, I did not abuse this practice and my health was but the better for it.

I thus reached my eighteenth year. Though I say it myself I had become truly beautiful.

I was above middle-height, my hair abundant and of a lovely dark chestnut colour, my eyes brown, very sparkling and provided with long lashes. My mouth was a little large and extremely sensual but was set off with pretty teeth; a black beauty spot on the right side of my upper lip added to my charms. I had admirable shoulders, breasts full, firm and well placed, a figure supple and slender and buttocks voluminous but well proportioned. My mound of Venus was finely shaped and without having the rare fleece of my aunt, I was well provided in this matter. By a singular peculiarity, this pretty fur was silky and very short.

How many times, dear Lucien, have you placed me in a manner to enjoy this view! What caresses! What kisses! But we must not anticipate. Let us add, to finish this portrait that I had firm hands and very elegant feet. All this made of me a morsel fit for a king.

My grandmother at this time felt that her end was near and she was concerned for my future so, without letting me know, she sought a husband for me.

One day an old friend of hers visited and made a proposal to her which seemed to crown her hopes and dearest desires. Here it is.

M. de Cornylle was presented to us. He was twenty-eight years of age, had much distinction of manners, a handsome shape, and a well-made figure.

His family was of the old aristocracy and his large fortune made him an excellent match. He had not as manly an air as M. de Vycabre, but such as he was, he greatly pleased me and I gave him my heart from the very first day.

As for him, immediately he perceived me he was bewitched. We were both of one mind; accordingly two months later we were married.

We were to due to pass some time at my grandmother's and afterwards go to Paris, where my husband had an employment.

Helene and her husband came to assist me at my marriage.

She was, as always, pretty and happy; I gave her my little confidences and told her that I was disposed to love my husband with all my heart, and that but one thing chagrined me and that was that I found him a little cold and reserved, although always affectionate and gallant.

Helene began to laugh and assured me that all this would be speedily changed.

The great day arrived – Madame Vycabre took the place of another and attired me herself.

As the evening arrived I was consumed with desire – and also with inexpressible fear; the act I was about to accomplish, although well known to me in theory, gave me terrible apprehension.

At last, the evening ended and Helene carried me off to the nuptial chamber!

It was her own! It was on this bed that I had seen her so well feasted, that I was become a fully fledged woman.

Helene put me to bed and, seating herself close to me, proceeded to instruct me in matters of which she thought I would be profoundly ignorant. With sensitivity and tact, she explained the whole matter to me very clearly. Then she kissed me, recommended that I comply with all my husband' desires, wished me courage and withdrew.

An instant afterward M. de Cornylle entered, clad in a dressing gown. He came to the bed, kissed me with ardour, said some very affectionate things to me, took off his garment and came into bed.

Charles, for that was his name, pressed me in his arms; the contact of his nude limbs against mine made me thrill. He kissed me sweetly, at the same time telling me not to be afraid, and drew still closer to me. I was now trembling all over – I dared not speak and yet I desired – he whispered to me:

'Would you like to have a little baby?' And at the same time his right knee insinuated itself between my thighs and separated them. I resisted at first, then yielded a little, then further. Speedily Charles drew closer. I now felt the point of the object I so much desired.

The first contact had on me the effect of gunpowder; all the heat of my temperament rushed to the spot about to be attacked and I almost came! But Charles aimed badly, either too high or too low – I was breathless, on fire, yet I dared not guide his movements!

At last I felt him at the right spot, at the entrance. He thrust vigorously, a keen pain seized me, I gave a start and drew back.

Disconcerted, Charles asked my pardon and implored me to have a little courage. He resumed his place. I no longer budged, and taking a little more advantageous position, I determined to suffer anything to finish it more quickly.

It seemed to me that Charles did not manage with much virility and I felt that there was a great difference in the size of the instrument that was now perforating me and that of M. de Vycabre. Moreover, he did not speak to me, did not say any of those things overheard by me, and which I believed could not be separated from the operation we were performing.

At last Charles seemed to gather a little more strength and gave a solid thrust – I imitated him, at the same time stiffening myself. The pain caused me to cry out, but I had the satisfaction of feeling myself penetrated, for his entire instrument was now in me.

For a moment my husband continued his movement back and forth, then he quivered, uttered several sighs and remaining motionless. I now felt the warm liquor flood me and diminish a little the roasting pain that was devouring me.

Charles withdrew and stretched himself at my side, visibly fatigued. While as for me, despite my desires and imagination I had not experienced any pleasure. I was not astonished at this as Helene had already warned me that it would be so.

Charles kissed me and then wished me good night, turned his back on me and promptly went to sleep.

I remained very much astonished and embarrassed. I was willing to recommence and, in spite of my pain, I was quite ready to do so. At last I made up my mind it was no use in waiting so I went to sleep in my turn.

I awoke late the next morning; much to my surprise, I was alone. Suddenly Charles came out of the dressing room and approached me. He was already dressed. He kissed me on the forehead, said some affectionate words to me, enquired whether I had slept well, but all was cold.

My heart, ready to fly towards him, stood still; it seemed to me that he should have stayed with me till I woke in order to press me in his arms, to speak to me of love and happiness – in short to recommence his caresses of the evening before.

I felt that I should have responded to his transports and that no apprehension of pain would have restrained me from receiving him. In short, a doubt as to my future tightened in my breast. This was not what I had dreamt of.

Charles quitted the room saying that he would leave me to dress myself. I did not even think of doing so and buried myself in sad reflections. A loving voice called me and Helene ran in to kiss me.

I flung my arms around her neck, embraced her and burst into tears.

'What is it then? Bon Dieu! dear child!' she said to me.

In truth I should have been much embarrassed to reply; it would have been impossible for me to articulate my grief. This was not my dream of love and I felt that the ardent fire that burned within me would not find the release it so urgently sought.

Helene thought that I was simply experiencing a nervous moment and she exerted herself to calm me by joking with me, soon the natural gaiety of my character came to the surface, I arose and plunged into the bath that my maid had drawn for me.

The day passed pleasantly; everybody around me was happy and my husband seemed to be enchanted. He was gallant and as tender as his nature allowed him to be, this put me at my ease and I returned his caresses less timidly.

The night came and he carried me off to bed early, less constrained himself than the night before. He pressed me in his arms and told me that he loved me and kissed me very tenderly. I ventured to say to him that I also loved him and I gave him a kiss that electrified him, for I felt something hard pressing against my thigh that seemed to promise me some satisfaction.

As on the evening before, he bent to my ear and whispered:

'Do you want us to repeat what we did last night?

I did not reply but could not prevent myself from opening my thighs and furtively drawing up my chemise. He placed himself on me. I put my arms around his neck, waiting for the moment impatiently.

I speedily felt the head of his instrument and I profited by his agitation to introduce it as far as possible in me. A lively enough pain was still produced but I did not stop there, pleasure and the fire that raced through my veins made me forget the discomfort. I already felt the forerunners of enjoyment and I put a check on myself in order not to speak – to say what I really felt.

I now understood perfectly the words of my aunt, but the silence of Charles, who seemed concentrated entirely on himself, prevented my giving vent to my feelings.

Charles continued his movements and kissed me, but he did not seem to be transported out of himself as I could have wished.

However I was now very happy, it seemed to me that I was melting away. I could not prevent myself from giving a thrust of the loins and uttering an exclamation. Now I remained motionless – I enjoyed even losing consciousness – Charles stopped, seemingly astonished at my transports; I restrained myself and he went on again.

What more shall I say? He was a long time with this sweet business, and I shed the sweet celestial dew four times! At last I felt him tremble, and sigh and a jet of flame inundated me inside.

We both lay still. I was exalted and ready to begin again; he was broken and, desiring only slumber, slept!

PART II

On awakening, the next morning, I found myself alone. I was not displeased and thought over the whole scene of the night before.

I was curious to inspect myself so, sitting on a pillow, my legs well apart, I examined my gaping interior. I found that my entire finger penetrated it with ease. This inspection amused me and would have certainly produced results had not a discreet knock on the door made me hasten to cover myself up, and I resumed a decent position.

My visitor was Helene. She found me fresh and gay and, after kissing me, we chatted like two sisters while I dressed.

My pretty aunt treated me as a woman and invited my confidences which I did not refuse her. When I told her that I had spent four times, while Charles had delivered himself of a single emission, she made an impatient movement; it was very evident that the paucity of my husband's virile force compared with my own, surprised her.

The day passed; my husband, a keen sportsman, went shooting game and, for my part, I went out walking with Helene. Dinner united us and, in the evening, we played music until it was time to retire.

This was the third night of our married life. Ah, what a difference from the two preceding ones! Charles put a frightful silk handkerchief around his head, spoke of our approaching departure and of our homecoming, but did not say one word of love, or give me any caresses. He kissed me coldly, turned over and went to sleep.

I awoke early the next morning and was seized with a desire to examine the male instrument which I had already felt twice and which I suspected was very different from that of M. de Vycabre.

Circumstances favoured me, it was warm, Charles had thrown back the sheet and by good luck his shirt was somewhat rucked up. I pushed the sheet still further down and then, with infinite care, moved so as to see that sorrowful tool that was my only source of consolation.

In truth what a difference, there was from that of M. de Vycabre – little, stunted – in a wrinkled skin, scarcely could one perceive the presence of its flabby head reposing on his thigh; and from that moment on I believe our fate was fixed.

Charles made a movement, I hastened to turn round and pretended to be asleep. He got out of bed first, as usual.

Thus the period of our sojourn with my grandmother approached its end and we began our proper married life together. Certainly I was not happy, though my husband loved me as much as his cold nature would permit. My beauty enchanted him and he refused me nothing that I could wish for, but all this did not suffice me. It was not this that I had dreamt of. I desired an ardent love, voluptuous and lascivious, for which I was ideally suited, but I saw before me a gentle, monotonous life – probably childless, and far too bloodless for one of my temperament.

Charles gave himself to me once or twice a week, always with the same helpless reserve. He only kissed me on my cheeks and forehead – my breasts so firm and fresh, never received his caresses; his hands seemed to fly away from the charming spot between my thighs that would have so eagerly welcomed his attentions. As for me, I did not dare to touch him, as I was sure that I would have been repulsed.

We had been married two years. I was now twenty years of age, my temperament had become more passionate in every way, while that of my husband seemed to have lost some of its force; I had not had a child, consequently nothing had changed my ideas.

By now my grandmother was dead and we lived in Paris. My husband's position obliged him to often beg leave of absence for several days at a time which, moreover, accorded with his sporting tastes.

I was thus often left alone and, in spite of my passion for music, which I had cultivated with some measure of success, my head often grew disordered, and my over-excited senses presented to me nothing but scenes of love and delirium.

What nights I have passed when alone! I have instinctively writhed myself into the most lascivious positions, that you could possibly imagine.

My finger was no longer enough to satisfy my desires. I pressed my bolster and entwined my arms about it, clasping it in my arms as well as though it could bring me joy. I rubbed myself furiously against it and arrived at a degree of relative enjoyment but this did not suffice except to still further increase my longings.

I changed postures, placing myself astride it; I rubbed myself anew until the wellsprings of pleasure, swollen by this stimulant, finally opened themselves and procured me some relief.

These nervous excitements gave me hallucinations, the nature of which were shaped by my frenetic state; my sweet and gay character became capricious. For a time I resisted but finally, I succumbed; was I then very culpable?

I often saw Madame D . . ., the wife of the Chief Magistrate of the town. She was a little blonde who had once been very beautiful but she was already on the turn. I believed that she had had many adventures in her youth.

One day, having gone to make a call on her, she informed me that M. Formatey had come to take command of the garrison. She said he was a young officer who had been much and well spoken of, who had fought with great distinction, and had been promoted very rapidly until he held the commission of Lieutenant Colonel; that he was about thirty-six years old and unmarried.

Madame told me that she had invited him to dinner, and she then invited my husband and myself for the same day. Was it a presentiment that I had? I do not know, but I returned home very thoughtful, even feeling a spark of jealousy towards Madame D . . .

The dinner took place three days later; I had made, I must admit it, a most ravishing toilette.

We entered the room and found M. Formatey there before us; in a moment I had taken stock of him. He was a tall, vigorous and strapping fellow, with a free and open physiognomy and distinguished manners. He was introduced and his sweet and charming voice vibrated within my heart.

I felt a chill, then the blood all rushed to my head. Oh, I was captured all right! I did not even seek to fight the feelings that invaded my entire being.

We sat down to dinner, which was very lively and M. Formatey shone by his quick wit. He was at the right of Madame D . . . who flirted with him. I could have slain her.

After dinner he approached me and begged my permission to call, then chatted with my husband who was pleased greatly with him.

Madame D . . . went to the piano and played a waltz. Monsieur D . . . said that I waltzed well and solicited me to take a turn with him but, he being somewhat elderly and somewhat feeble, fatigue speedily told on him and M. Formatey presented himself to fill his place.

When his arm encircled my waist, I was seized with a nervous movement which did not escape him, and I very imprudently allowed myself to be carried away by the delicious sensation.

M. Formatey boldly profited by it and, while turning the corner of the room, he found a means to press me so closely to him that I felt for an instant against my stomach an object so hard and stiff, that I thought I should faint. Ah, this waltz was all that was needed to complete my defeat!

All too speedily the happy evening came to an end. On returning home, I undressed myself promptly, said good night to my husband and, under pretext of being tired, lay down with my buttocks turned toward Charles.

As it chanced, a caprice took him, and I felt him gently raise my chemise. Then, pressing me towards himself, he sought to put it into me from behind. For a moment I was disinclined but, within a moment, my temperament got the upper hand and I lent myself to his desires. He, however, fumbled at me clumsily and failed to gain an entry.

I lost my patience and, hurling the clothes down to the foot of the bed, I seized his reluctant dart and buried it within me to the hilt.

At this moment I scarcely thought of poor Charles, in my imagination Formatey had taken his place. I imagined that it was he who was moving behind me and in my mind I addressed to him everything that I could have wished to say if he had really been there.

Three times my amorous dew was shed for him and him

alone, as the result of my thoughts my husband profited without knowing it, and behaved a little better than usual refreshing me with a more abundant shower of moisture.

When he withdrew I feared that, with his usual habitual ridiculous reserve, he would be displeased with the spontaneous impulse which had made me seize and imprison his instrument myself. On the contrary he appeared to take it kindly and I remembered it for the future.

The next day, when M. Formatey called to pay us a visit, we were out. I was really chagrined to find his card. The day after he called again, this eagerness pleased me very much, we received him in our best style and pressed him to come often.

It seemed to me that he regarded me with a particular sentiment and I was as happy as could be.

A tender intimacy was not slow in establishing itself between us and my love grew greater day by day. I knew that my adored Formatey already shared it. Up to now he had said nothing, but I was sure of it. What woman ever deceived herself in this?

We never found ourselves alone: I ardently desired, but at the same time dreaded, this moment. I did not wish to deliver myself up to him entirely at the first encounter yet I felt that it would be impossible to resist for a single moment. I made a resolution to know him better but, unhappily, my strength deserted me completely as soon as I saw him.

In such a state how could I have resisted his attack?

One day he called about three o'clock in the afternoon. My husband was absent, but I had a very tiresome lady visitor who could not make up her mind to go.

I saw my dear Formatey suffering as he waited and, not being able to decently remain any longer, at last he started to leave, darting at me a glance that I could not resist. I said to him:

'Did not my husband promise you a book?'

'Yes, Madame. And I had hoped to get it today.'

'If you will wait. I will go and get it for you.'

'Will you excuse me, Madame?' I said to my eternal visitor, 'will you permit me to leave you alone for a moment?'

She replied, 'Oh, yes, willingly!'

We were in my little room. Formatey, who understood my little ruse, went out and waited for me in the next room, where I joined him with some book or other in my hand.

In an instant he declared his love for me. What did he say? What did I reply to him?

I know nothing, I remember nothing. I conducted him to the entrance door, fearing that someone would hear him; there was a double door between where we stood and a little ante-chamber where the servant was sitting.

M. Formatey seized me in his arms, half opened my lips and imprinted a kiss, a long kiss of fire, a kiss which re-echoed through my entire being and arrested the protest which I should have uttered in spite of myself.

At the same instant, his eager hand had raised my petticoats and his finger knowledgeably caressed my burning cleft which left, quick as lightning, a palpable mark of its pleasure on his invading hand.

'Go – go – go! Do leave me!' I implored in a stifled voice. 'Go! go! – Tomorrow, three o'clock!' And I fled in a state that I can hardly describe.

Happily, the lady visiting me was very near-sighted and did not perceive my disorder.

I will not attempt to relate my impressions until the next afternoon – the only thing that I can recall is that I was determined.

Fortunately my husband had to be away, so I arranged things in such a manner that my servants were sent on errands; I made a fresh toilette and then waited. My dear Formatey arrived, I opened the door for him myself, and led him into my boudoir.

We seated ourselves, both sufficiently embarrassed, and he very respectfully begged my pardon for what he had done the day before, telling me that he had not been his master at the moment when the delicious movement had seized him; and that his love for me was such that he would die if he could not have me.

I did not know what to reply, my heart was so full – he took my hand and kissed it. I arose, trembling, our mouths met, and, I confess, I no longer made any resistance! I had not the strength. I tasted unknown happiness, I felt him draw me close. What should we do?

There was nothing in my boudoir but an uncomfortable settee, and some common chairs.

All the time holding me in his arms, Formatey seated himself upon a chair in such a manner that I found myself standing in front of him and bending over his body.

I felt one of his arms leave my waist and speedily my clothes were lifted up in front as my handsome lover sought to pass his knees between my legs.

'Oh, not that!' I said between spasms. 'No, I pray you – not that, have pity!'

Without taking any notice of my feeble protestations of expiring modesty, Formatey made efforts to bend me in such a way that I should be astride of him; instinctively, although desiring it all the time, I resisted, refusing to bend – thus we exhausted ourselves.

At last, having lowered my eyes a little, I saw a spectacle which at once terminated the struggle. My conqueror had already produced his instrument quite ready for the fray; its haughty and rubicund head raised itself arrogantly – its length and thickness truly exceptional, rendering it far superior even to that of M. de Vycabre.

At this sight I no longer had the strength or desire to resist. My thighs opened themselves of their own accord, I let myself sink whilst hiding my head on my lover's shoulder, and I abandoned myself to him, opening myself as wide as possible, desiring yet fearing the entrance of so fine a guest.

I speedily felt the head between the lips of my grotto which, following the puny tool of my husband, was not used to such a treat. I made a movement to aid him and had scarcely introduced the point, when a burning jet of amorous liquor covered my thighs and stomach.

The prolonged waiting and the excitement had caused the precious dew to gush forth much too quickly for me and so I was not able to enjoy as I had hoped.

I could not prevent myself from letting my disappointment be seen, but my lover, covering me with kisses, told me that he needed but to wait for an instant and that I should speedily be more content with him.

We sat down on the settee and, entwined in each other's arm, we spoke to the full of our love and happiness. We had loved each other at the first sight it seemed and so had yielded to an irresistible passion.

At the end of several minutes, I saw that my lover was ready to recommence and I asked myself how we were going to do it!

I did not wish to try again the posture that had failed us so dismally. I noticed that Formatey was also looking about him; then I had an idea, I got up, smiling at him, and urged him to do the same.

I stepped back and he pursued me; at last I leaned forward nonchalantly against the mantelpiece and presented to him my behind my croup, which I made undulate with a cat-like movement, at the same time I looked back at him, darting him a provocative glance. Ah, I was understood. Formatey sprang towards me and gave me a kiss, while saying:

'Thanks!' Then he placed himself behind me and he raised my petticoats up over my loins.

On perceiving my rounded and quivering posterior, he uttered a cry of admiration. I was waiting, but was not expecting the homage which I received.

The great fool threw himself on his knees; then, after covering my buttocks with kisses, he opened them below and I felt lips and tongue! In my turn I uttered a cry and nearly swooned away.

Formatey raised himself and commenced to put inside me his priapus, his enormous priapus. Despite our united efforts, this was not easy, so he withdrew and, putting a little saliva on it, I then speedily felt myself penetrated – filled. I was in a state of inexpressible ecstasy.

Bending over me, my lover glued his lips to mine, which I made possible by bending my head. His tongue caressed mine and I lost control of my senses. As the supreme moment arrived I became crazed with passion and cried out in broken and unfinished words of love.

Formatey restrained himself and beamed at my happiness. He allowed me to calm down and then I felt his sweet movements commence again. Ah, how well he knew how to give pleasure and even to double it by a thousand delicious shades! Oh, this first lesson, I can feel it yet!

'Dear Angel!' he said, 'express your feelings, it is good to utter those sweet confidences, when we become one person as we are at this moment.'

Oh, how happy this speech made me. I who had always desired to utter those words with which my ears had been so delicately struck at Pauvanne, when a similar scene had been enacted by my aunt and her lover. I did not need another invitation.

'I am coming – again – I say again, – finish me! I am co-m-ing! Ah! Ah!'

'My adored one, I am coming also! Ah – oh – here I come!'

Formatey gave a vigorous thrust of the loins and sank upon me – I felt his emissions and almost lost consciousness again.

How was it that I could stand his embrace? Nothing of what I had imagined on seeing my aunt, could approach this reality. I was swooning, my head between my hands, my bosom palpitating, incapable of making another movement.

As Formatey withdrew from me, I was still coming, I had been coming all the time! In spite of myself, I remained uncovered up to the waist, trembling, mechanically continuing to undulate my buttocks which caused the overflow of ambrosia to fall to the ground.

My lover had pity on me. After rapidly putting himself to rights, he lowered my petticoats and, taking me in his arms, he sat me beside himself on the settee.

For a moment my mind wandered, he calmed me, his sweet voice brought me to my senses a little. I begged him to leave me to myself for a time and he retired.

I now took stock of myself. I was in an incredible state of disorder. I had to change my linen, my chemise and stockings were not only stained with the amorous liquor but smeared with drops of blood, for it was not with impunity that I had consorted with a member of that size.

When I regained something of a semblance of order, in ideas as well as toilette, I flung myself on my bed and slept profoundly. My husband would not return till late in the evening and I woke up about seven o'clock, fresh and strong as I had not felt for some time.

I gave way to reflection. I had been carried away by an irresistible sentiment and, above all, by a natural need, as necessary for my nourishment as food.

It was certainly not that I was vicious; I loved my husband as a friend, as the companion of my existence, and if he had the necessary virile forces which were so indispensable to me, or even if he had sought to augment them with skilful caresses, I should never have dreamt of being unfaithful to him. I resolved to save him from all pain and I have fully succeeded – he had never had the slightest suspicion.

This resolution demanded much skill. The circle of acquaintances with which I was surrounded, were exceedingly active in scandal-mongering and I had to take excessive precautions to conceal my liaison.

I warned my lover and knew that I could count on his honour, and he did everything on his part to preserve my reputation.

Several days passed without our seeing each other; I suffered much from this and he as much as I. A gesture, a look while walking or in company with others was all that we had for consolation for eight long days.

At last Formatey could hold out no longer. He came to pay us a visit; my husband was at home. We chatted in a friendly manner, someone else came to call, he took his leave and my husband went to the door with him and returned to the room with our new visitor.

I do not know what instinct warned me that Formatey

had not gone out of the house, but I excused myself as the visitor was talking business with my husband, and I went into the ante-chamber.

I had not deceived myself. Formatey had not left; seeing that there was no servant in sight, he was still standing inside the entrance.

On seeing me, he threw himself upon me, pressing me in his arms with violent passion.

'Dear Angel, how I am suffering and how long a time it has been.'

'And I have found it so, too!' I replied.

We were still standing between the doors and before I had time to think, our lips were glued together, my clothes were pulled up to the waist, his finger had penetrated into my burning cave which opened itself under his pressure and, my hand had seized his dear member. What more can I say? Several moments passed and I gasped for breath, withdrawing my hand to find it entirely bathed in a warm and abundant liquor.

We made our escape in opposite directions.

Several days then passed and we were unable to join one another, then at last a happy moment of liberty arrived and we had an hour to ourselves.

Ah, how we profited by it! My lover appeared in my little room. I flew to meet him, I ate him up with kisses and caresses.

'Let us do it quickly!' We both exclaimed in a single breath, 'let us profit by this chance for happiness.'

I tore myself from his arms, flung up my skirts from behind and, placing myself on my knees on the settee, presented my buttocks to him. I swooned with pleasure from the fury of his consequent attack.

Then we seated ourselves but my lover was not contented

and, in spite of my fears, I could not stop him. He placed himself on his knees between my legs, which he had me open widely; I took into my hand his vigorous firebrand which had already regained all its hardness, I caressed it a moment, then I buried it in myself gradually.

When the arrow had completely disappeared within its quiver, Formatey bent over me, raised my legs on his arms, threw me backwards and then thrust so energetically that a second ejaculation soon exploded within me.

My aim is not to relate day by day all that took place at our various meetings. I will merely confine myself to describing the most stirring doings of this adorable liaison, which I could have wished to last forever.

My lover knew how to vary the pleasure without ever arriving at satiety; he found a singular voluptuousness in teaching me the arts of enjoying, and he had in me the most docile of pupils.

He taught me the real names of things, making me say them many times, but only on the frenzy of passion. He only employed them himself in the supreme transports; he claimed, and rightly, that it was a spice of high taste, which one should not abuse, for fear that it would lose all its flavour.

It will doubtless come to me to forget myself some time in sweet remembrances, but after all, what does it matter?

What refined caresses, what lascivious positions he was able to teach me! What caprices, what childishnesses on both sides were realized as soon as thought of! I made much progress under so good a master, that I eventually surpassed him.

I greatly delighted in changing the method thus sometimes, when ridden from behind which was one of his favourite postures, I would unhorse my rider and fly to the end of the room. There I would place myself on a chair, my legs in the air, presenting my open pussy. Scarcely had my lover penetrated me than I would, in a new caprice, seat myself on top of him, burying his tool to the utmost within me.

My dear Mimi! It was thus that I ordinarily called my splendid champion who gave me so much pleasure and which had now become a passion to me. I could never tire of admiring its length, its thickness, its marvellous stiffness: I played with it, I ate it up, I pumped it, caressed it in a thousand ways. I rubbed it against my titties, shut it up between them by pressing them together with both hands and often, when closed in this voluptuous channel, there it would shed its dew.

My lover returned all my caresses with interest, my pussy was his god, his idol. He assured me that no woman ever possessed one more beautiful than mine – he half opened it, he tickled it in a thousand ways. His greatest happiness consisted of putting his lips to it to suck it, to extract from it (so to speak) the quintessence of voluptuousness by titillations of the tongue which nearly drove me mad.

I had acquired such taste for practice that we seldom had a rendezvous without Formatey pleasuring me this way. I would throw myself down on a large sofa chair placed in my boudoir for just that purpose. There I would arrange myself with legs stretched out and raised on the arms of the chair.

My lover would fall on his knees in front of me, and perform his delicious *minette* – it was thus that he called this way of making love. When I began to writhe in paroxysms of pleasure, he would enter me and locked in each other's arms, we would enjoy each other to the point of madness.

Sometimes I would place myself on my knees on the settee and my lover would glue his face between my buttocks and pleasure me with his mouth from the rear – an activity which filled us both with transports of joy.

One day, after a long separation, my dear Formatey was at last able to see me alone! Alas! A monthly obstacle rendered our habitual pleasures impossible. I saw the pain on his face as he looked at my hand supplicatingly.

Certainly I was quite disposed to accord him that means of solace, in fact I had already had it in mind to do so, when a foolish idea popped into my head and I recalled the last scene between M. de Vycabre and my aunt in the park.

The conditions were identical and I wished to reproduce it in all this details. I easily prevailed upon Formatey to rise, placed him as I wanted and proceeded to manipulate his big tool in the same fashion as Helene had. I also managed to make my lover say the same words that M. de Vycabre had uttered on that memorable occasion.

At last he came and his dew gushed freely, the last pearls of which I collected in my handkerchief.

When it was finished I could not prevent myself from laughing and he asked my reasons. To this I replied thoughtlessly:

'Nothing, I just remembered something!'

At these words I saw his face darken and I quickly understood my mistake and the suspicions that I had raised in his mind against me. Not wishing to give him even the shadow of anxiety, I made him sit beside me and told him all that had happened before my marriage. This recital amused him greatly and he had me go into great detail. When I told him how I had managed to get satisfaction for myself, he cried:

'Ah, dearest, what would I not have given to have seen you in your turn tickle your delicious little clitoris.'

He continued asking me a lot of questions about my solitary customs and I even finished by telling him that, the day of our meeting at Madame D . . .'s house, I was so full of the remembrance of him that in the night I had done it for Charles but had thought only of HIM.

'Ah, indeed!' he replied to me, 'this is truly curious! Confidence for confidence, my dear angle, that very same evening and probably at the very same hour, we exchanged our souls in mutual enjoyment!'

'Is that true?'

'Listen, I returned home already more than half captivated by you; I had in fact loved you on seeing you; I had not yet had the happiness of enjoying your body but I regarded it as the aim of all my future efforts.

'I went to bed and thought only of you. I was in a state of – well, you can imagine – I extinguished my light and in my mind I covered your imaginary form with kisses of a delightful but not entirely satisfying sort. Then I did what you did, and the pleasure was such that I am now convinced that our discharges took place at the very same moment.'

'How can men then tickle themselves. Do they do it as we do?'

'Certainly we do; why should this natural means of relief be denied us? That which your pretty hand does, mine can do likewise.'

'Oh, how I would like to see that!'

'What, you want to . . .?'

'Yes, I want you to show me how to do it.'

'But you well know I do it just like you.'

'Well yes, but I pray you, give me this pleasure.'

While saying this, I uncovered the head of his instrument which, as a result of our talk, had regained its usual fine condition. I took his hand and placed it upon it.

'Now you are being silly.'

'No, sir, not at all, I wish it – do it quickly, and do it to the end, or I shall know that you do not love me any more.'

My lover did not know how to refuse me. After some hesitation he said: 'Oh very well, I agree but it is on the condition that as soon as it is possible, you will in your turn give me a demonstration of your pleasures when a young girl.'

'Oh, as to that, I will do it willingly, but now please go on.'

He soon did as I wished and, bending over him, I followed his movements one after the other with a singular sentiment to think of his pleasure and my curiosity.

Soon I had pity on him, I undid my corsage, and going on my knees in front of him, I finished the good work between my titties.

A short time after this caprice, my lover demanded the like of me. He recalled the promise I had made him and, in spite of a certain shame which had taken possession of me, I lent myself to his pleasure and stretched myself on the settee.

'No, not like that, you placed me to your liking, now it is my turn.'

'But what do you want?'

'You will see. Place yourself on this chair – like that-very well, now uncover your little pussy and tickle it with your left hand.'

Though puzzled, I obeyed. By now, Formatey had unclasped my corsage and stripped me to the waist. My lascivious instincts now kindled, what I had at first taken in hand as a joke I now began to take very seriously indeed.

Then I felt Formatey, who had placed himself behind me, insinuate his engine under my right arm. The originality of this fantasy inflamed my lustful imagination. I bent my head and avidly contemplated his handsome tool, whose helmet appeared and disappeared at each thrust of my dear lover who, for his part, had his eyes fixed on my left hand, which was by now working at its best.

Very soon our sighs mingled, we mutually warned each other, and our discharges took place at the same instant.

Some delicious months rolled by and our passion, far from weakening, or blunting our sensibilities from its frequency, only caused our love to grow more intense.

The precautions that we had taken with so much care assured us secrecy, and only once were we nearly surprised. We believed ourselves certain not to be disturbed, my husband was away, and I had sent my servants on errands at some distance.

After a chat and some caresses, I had made my lover understand my desires, and he had me placed to his liking, my body thrown back in my easy chair, my legs well apart and thus he commenced his adorable licking. I was ready to come, my eyes were closed, I was thinking only of myself and tasting one by one the delicious sensations his tongue was creating when all at once we heard steps on the stairs and voices in the next room.

Quick as lightning, we both jumped up, set our clothes to rights and sat ourselves at a proper distance when my maid, returning sooner than I had expected, opened the door and announced a lady of the town.

I was so terribly stunned that I could not move but the coolness and presence of mind on the part of my lover, who fortunately knew the lady, gave me time to compose myself and we were saved!

* * *

STATES OF ECSTASY

The fine weather arrived and I had to go to a spa a little distance from my hometown. I dreaded it, for I thought it would separate me from my lover, and Formatey was in despair. However, my husband insisted upon it and, as you may imagine, we did not wish to admit the real reason for my reluctance.

My husband could not accompany me, his occupation kept him at home, but he arranged to visit me frequently and to join me for a longer time as soon as he was able.

As for Formatey, it would be too imprudent to have received him.

I set off full of vexation, and passed the early days of my stay very quietly.

At the end of the first week, my husband came to see me and told me that shortly he would bring Formatey and two other friends to pass the day. Hope sprang anew, and I waited with feverish impatience.

At last, six days later, I received a letter that this trip had been fixed for the next day.

Having set out the day before, the gentlemen arrived at four o'clock in the morning. My husband came at once to find me and lay down by my side. Absence had awakened his rare desires, and although I anticipated being feasted by my dear Formatey, I should here avow that I willingly lent myself to Charles's wishes.

I clasped him in my arms, slipped my hand under his shirt and, taking his instrument, I gently worked it up with my fingers for a few seconds: then, having put it in its finest state of erection, I introduced it into my grotto.

Charles performed better than usual and swore to me that the caresses of my hand had made him experience the liveliest sensation of pleasure. Since then I have often made use of this means to excite him for my own satisfaction and sometimes even at his own request. We then slept until nine o'clock.

We went to breakfast at the hotel dining room with the gentlemen; the meal was an excellent one and we were all very gay. My dear Formatey sparkled with wit and verve. We could only communicate with our eyes but this language was well understood by us, and the message read, as plain as day, when can we meet alone?

It was my husband who unwittingly fixed matters for us. He proposed a lunch party in the woods and declared that after having conducted me back to the house, he would return to the hotel to lie down and recover from the fatigue of the ride the night before.

Formatey declared that he would employ that time in seeing some old friends; and the others said that they were going to visit the baths.

One glance exchanged with my lover was sufficient for me to understand him and, at noon when my husband was fast asleep at the hotel, Formatey slipped into my chamber.

Knowing his taste I had made a seductive toilette with a piquant head dress and donned rose-coloured stockings and fine slippers. I was clad only in a light peignoir, which my lover called a *foutoir*. I waited with impatience and was delirious the moment he appeared and devoured him with kisses.

'Ah, here you are at last, my dear angel, my dear love! Oh, how I have longed for you, come to my arms that I may devour you!

I closed the door and drew him towards the bed.

'Oh, come to my arms, seeing it's been two weeks without you! I thought I should die – how I have suffered!'

'And I, my darling, I have scarcely lived! We have not much time, let us profit by the opportunity quickly before some one comes to interrupt us.'

'Oh yes, we will, I am entirely yours to do with as you wish.'

As I finished these words, my peignoir was already on the floor. My lover undressed himself, then arranged me on the edge of the bed, placing two pillows behind me. Then he caressed and sucked my titties for some time, before raising my chemise and applying his burning lips to my hungry pussy which received this caress with a spasm of happiness.

'Ah, my darling,' I said, 'ah, I am spending already – it is coming again! – Ah, what delight! Oh, you are slaying me! Me now – come, put it into me – come, poke me!'

Formatey raised himself, lifted my legs up on his arms and began to thrust steadily into me. As for me, I was lying back softly and I followed his sweet activity with langorous eyes.

'Do it gently, slowly!' I said, 'let us be very long about it! Ah, how very good it is! It penetrates me to the heart! Ah! I am dying! Stop – slow down! stop a – little! Ah, I'm there, I am doing it – I am coming!'

'I, also, ah, I cannot hold out any longer, my darling, my *fouteuse*, I am coming – I give-you – my – semen!'

I remained swooning, but unsatisfied. My lover was still stretched out upon me, I had encircled his head with both arms and glued my mouth to his.

'Ah,' I whispered, 'you have done it much too quickly!'

'I could not stop myself – but do not move!'

'What do you want to do then?' was the question I naturally asked.

'You see that I am remaining inside you.'

'But I am all flooded, can't you see?'

'What does it matter, I am going to poke you again without leaving your sheath.'

'But is it possible?'

'You will see – how adorable your titties are, my darling. Give me your tongue, nicely now, – ah, that is like it! Move your dear bottom sweetly! There it is, wakening me up – can't you feel it?'

'Yes, it is returning – I can hold out no longer – I am doing it again! Start again, more quickly! I am dying – I am going mad – I'm doing it – I'm fuc . . . I'm doing it all the time, are you ready?'

'It's coming! I'm coming again. There – there it is!'

And a second discharge came to mingle itself with the first. For a time we remained in a swoon, then Formatey, lowering my legs, withdrew from me and a veritable deluge of amorous liquor fell to the floor.

I raised myself then and squeezed my lover in my arms, 'Ah, now happy I have been, I have spent as I have never spent before; and almost without a second's interruption.'

It was imperative for us to clear away all traces of our excesses; my thighs and stomach were literally covered with the sweet liquor. I had no bathroom but could not remain in such a condition so, taking my wash basin and telling Formatey to turn away, I made ablutions.

My lover, far from obeying me, did not refrain from devouring every single motion of mine and, as I finished, he took me in his arms and with my clothes thrown up, he smothered me with kisses and said: 'I want to poke you again!'

'Oh no, pray, you will make yourself ill.'

'Here, look it is again in full erection.'

The sight was all that was necessary to finish sending me mad. I flung myself on my knees, seized the beautiful rubicund head in my mouth and sucked it in delirium – when all at once I heard steps in the passage.

I sprang up and with one bound was at the door, looking

through the keyhole, for if it were my husband, we were lost. Happily I was mistaken and I motioned to Formatey, that it was all right, but remained watching and, with my eye at the keyhole stood in such a position that my naked buttocks were thrust up in the air. In a second my lover was behind me and before I had time to protest – even if I were so minded – I was penetrated from behind afresh, stormed by this adorable instrument which did not seem to want to rest! Oh, how I urged him on by opening and closing my buttocks, by writhing and panting – but enough . . .

The time had passed like lightning, so I sent my lover away, hastily remade the bed and put on a walking costume. Scarcely had I finished when my husband came to fetch me. He found me flushed and animated; I told him that I had allowed myself to be overcome by the heat and I had been sleeping.

We went downstairs and I was saluted with joyous acclamation by the gentlemen, who paid me compliments on the freshness and good taste of my toilette. I stole a glance at Formatey and happily nothing in his appearance announced that anything extraordinary had happened to him. So we went outside.

The woods to which we went were deliciously fresh and beautiful and we soon reached a lodge where food had been prepared for us and the eating of it was the occasion of wild gaiety. They made me drink some champagne, of which I had a little need to make me feel exalted.

After lunch, we took a little stroll. My husband was chatting with Formatey while I walked along quietly by them, the two others having taken another road.

We soon arrived at a wild and awesome spot, filled with rocks and shaded by great trees. At this very moment one of the gentlemen far away from us called to my husband:

'Come quickly and look at this!'

Charles left us, running in the direction of his friends. Immediately he had disappeared from our sight, Formatey glued his mouth to mine.

'Dear angel,' he said, 'we must make the most of this opportunity.'

'Are you mad?'

'Oh, no, I simply love you to distraction, will you let me do it?'

'*Mon Dieu*, someone will surprise us and I shall be lost.'

'No, not if we hurry. Bend over.'

I did as I was told.

'Are you there?'

'There it is – it is going in.'

'Ah, do it quickly – I am all of a tremble.'

'There, darling – come! Come again!'

'Ah, it is done; now withdraw quickly.'

'Ah, *Mon Dieu*!'

My petticoats, which had been raised from behind, were scarcely lowered when we heard the party returning.

I went to meet them; they were coming to fetch us to observe a swarm of bees which were buzzing round the top of a tree.

We strolled back to the carriage and returned to the hotel. In the evening we had a dance in the drawing room of the establishment; then we bade one another adieu. The gentlemen left away early the next morning and my husband remained with me.

You can imagine what I was thinking when I returned home and spent the day in ordinary duties. On getting ready for bed, while I was busy arranging my head dress in front of the mirror my husband, enchanted by the day's outing, was gay and tender. I had put on a chemise which revealed the seductive charms of my buttocks from behind. I perceived that Charles was gazing at them and, as I watched him in the glass, I saw his eyes brighten.

'Well, well,' I said to myself, 'is it be possible that he is capable of doing me twice in the same day?'

Wishing to assure myself of it, I coquettishly took a pose which further exhibited what I knew to be one of my prime assets. Then, nonchalantly putting one foot on a chair, taking care that my chemise was lifted up more than was necessary. I took off my garter.

This manoeuvre succeeded. Charles, dressed only in his shirt, came to me, he kissed me on the neck, and put his hand between my buttocks.

'Stop!' I said to him, turning round and embracing him as I returned his kiss. 'What has got into you this evening?'

'My dear one, I find you very beautiful.'

'But am I not so, every day?'

'Yes, but this evening more than ever.'

'Well, what do you want? Let us see.' Saying this, I put my hand on his instrument, which stood up a little but was far from being in a fit state.

'You see that you cannot do anything.'

'Oh, but I pray you, caress it a little.'

'What is it then that excites it thus?''

'It's . . . that is . . .'

'What then?'

'The sight of your beautiful backsides.'

'Well then, you shalt not see them any more –' but, while saying this I, by a cat-like movement threw my clothes up in such a manner that the whole of my posteriors was revealed while the front of me was reflected in the mirror. At the same time my other hand had not let go of his tool. I soon had the satisfaction of feeling it harden. Wishing to profit by this situation, I made Charles sit down and seated myself astride him, but I speedily perceived that he had weakened and that the position I had taken would not be at all suitable to his tiny tool.

I raised myself, everything had to be done all over again. I was much too excited to attain my ends, so I recommenced the caress of my hand. I put into it all my skill and by his aid I at last had the satisfaction of seeing it, his weapon once more in its handsomest state. Then, drawing a chair near the glass, I placed one foot on it and the other on the floor and introduced Charles from behind.

Charles, carried away and beyond himself, did me in such a fashion as to make me come three times. As for him he took a long time succeeded after an effort in discharging, thanks to the smart movements of my buttocks and the talent I had acquired of tightening my sheath on his wretched instrument.

Finally we retired and went to sleep, both much fatigued.

Thus on this eventful day I had been caressed six times ! And as for myself – I do not exaggerate in saying that I had come more than twenty times. But such was the heat of my temperament and its aptitude for amorous combats, that I got up the next morning as fresh as if nothing out of the ordinary had taken place.

I returned home . . . and resumed my affair with my dear Formatey.

My husband rarely absented himself for more than a day at a time and so our pleasures were of no great duration simply brief instants snatched during the day. However, on occasion some indispensable journeys took place and we made the most of them.

One night, happy in the knowledge that we had several

hours of security, we decided to completely profit by our good fortune; my lover proposed that we undress ourselves and use my bed. I accepted with enthusiasm and soon he was lying on his back wearing nothing but his shirt, while I was unlacing myself.

I joined him, having nothing on but my chemise and stockings. He seized me in his arms and we embraced each other furiously. It was but a moment before my lover became jealous of the flimsy material that still covered me, and he drew off my remaining clothes in spite of the slight resistance that I made.

At first he contemplated my naked charms then he covered every inch of my body with burning kisses – I was delirious! I was mad!

I wished in my turn to render him the happiness which I had experienced, so I kissed with ardour every part of his beautiful, manly body. At a certain spot – a cherished jewel which stuck itself up in so fiery a manner I could have eaten it – I stopped and kissed and sucked.

In this posture my buttocks were almost turned to my lover's side. I felt him take hold of my left thigh and seek to make it pass beneath him.

'What do you want to do?' I asked, turning my head a little in order to see what he was at.

'Straddle.'

'But what do you want to do?'

'You will soon know. There, like that!' and I found myself astride his chest, my head still in the same place.

'No,' said he, 'lower yourself and push your beautiful backside a little forward; there – now place your pretty little vulva on my mouth.'

'I am there.'

'Let us both do *minette*; you will warn me so that we will come together.'

Although puzzled at this new fashion of getting pleasure, I lent myself to it with good grace. Speedily I felt his delicious tongue wandering in my pussy. I became wild – I took the instrument that I had left for a moment. I put its entire head into my mouth and pumped with frenzy!

An electric current seemed to shoot through my body; each blow of Formatey's tongue was returning to him by my suction. What pleasure! I had already come three times when I felt the fourth spend arriving with my lover also approaching the supreme pleasure, palpitating and quivering, so I said:

'I am there – I am coming!'

What happened I do not know, I swooned and nearly lost my senses under a burning jet of amorous liquid.

The adorable lessons my lover had taught me, rendered me very skilful. I thought I had nothing to learn, but I deceived myself for there remained one more a supreme lesson.

I have often stated that my buttocks or rather my backside was of rare beauty; the furrow which divided the oval had already received thousands of kisses from my lover, whose greatest pleasure was in placing me in such a position that he could thoroughly enjoy this spectacle.

He would partly then open the lips of my pussy, caressing and kissing it, feasting it in every manner – and sometimes his finger would mount a little higher and I felt a strange titillation at the secret spot placed just above.

Sometimes, when sworded up to the hilt and swooning under the celestial dew which he was darting into me, I had felt his finger penetrate very far into this narrow passage.

This singular caress had always given me a peculiar,

voluptuous feeling and I had not sought to analyse it.

On one of the rare evenings when we were able to sleep together after having caressed one another for a long time, my lover drew off my chemise and lovingly observed my naked form.

Knowing my passion for the unusual, he was always trying some new way and when I presented my bottom to him, opening myself to the utmost, expecting him to put it in as usual, Formatey contented himself with caressing me with the head of his priapus.

'Put it into me, then, you are making me die with a slow fire.'

'Wait a little yet.'

'Ah, what is it that you are doing to me? You are doing it wrong, it doesn't go in there!'

In fact I felt his point seeking to enter into this singular orifice of which I have just spoken.

'Let me do it so, my beloved one, I pray you; there should not remain a single spot in your beautiful body in which I have not deposited an offering.'

'But this it not possible, it will never enter.'

'Oh, yes, it shall enter entirely, if you will allow me to do it.'

'But you will kill me, I shall suffer so – I shall cry out – I shall not enjoy it.'

'Oh yes, you will and afterwards you shall say yourself that it was very good. I will even wager that you will ask me to do it again more than once.'

'No, it is impossible, put it in lower down, where you can do as you will.'

'But I beg you – it is the greatest proof of love that a woman can give. I implore you.'

'Ah, *Mon Dieu*, I cannot refuse you – come do it, but it is very singular.'

So I said nothing more and, remaining passive, presented my posterior in the best manner that I could. My lover went to my dressing table and lubricated himself with a cosmetic, then resuming his place he presented himself afresh at the entrance.

His first attempt did not succeed and instead of having the promised pleasure I felt only pains but I loved him so much that I would have suffered more. And apart from this, curiosity and the desire for the unknown sustained me.

My lover arrested his movement for a little and, passing his hand around in front of me, he started touching me.

The pleasure thus kindled demanded a second trial but my lover's position, bent over me, made it difficult for him to continue this caress, so he took my hand and put it where his had been. I comprehended and titillated myself.

I felt his terrible weapon afresh but the pleasure I was obtaining for myself neutralized the pain which my poor backside still felt. At last I felt as if a ring was dilating within me and, with another blow, the entire cylinder was sheathed entirely. I redoubled my movements and an immense, double - bitter - enjoyment invaded me. I nearly lost consciousness and fell forward, stretched in a spasm impossible to describe.

My lover happily was not unhorsed, he followed my movements and found himself stretched at full length upon me. He still gave several blows and filled his singular lodging place with a warm ejaculation thrust home with heavy sighs, witnesses of his vivid enjoyment.

We remained for a time in this position without speaking. I felt a certain shame that I could not explain and almost regretted that I had enjoyed it so much. On the other hand, I could not prevent myself from being enchanted with this new style of pleasure. Formatey kissed me and whispered:

'Eh, well, what do you say?'

'I don't know what to say.'

'Have you come?'

'Eh . . . yes . . .'

'Are you vexed at having yielded to my caprice? If I ask it again of you, will you . . .'

'Why yes, I believe that – well, yes, but not too often. It is too much!'

During this conversation we had remained with my lover's pin thrust into my dainty hole, I felt it become small, he tried to withdraw it but I tightened my buttocks to such a point that I held him willy nilly to his post.

'You wished to go in – now you will stay in.'

I had counted on his virility and whilst waiting for his revival, I excited him, using all the words he had taught me.

'What does you call this manner of fuck . . . poking?' I asked him, 'you know my poor cunt has received nothing?'

'Ah,' he interrupted, 'I feel my cock coming to life again shall I again feast on your backside?'

'Yes, dearest, I feel I have a taste for it – and I still want semen.'

And with this smuttiness, I clenched my buttocks gradually so as to give him liberty of action. I commenced to feel afresh the forerunners of the double enjoyment which I had already experienced but my lover did not seem to be ready, he seemed to me to be feeble, so we replaced ourselves in our former position, and I said:

'Now, my darling, don't you move just let me do everything.'

So I began to move my arse backward and forward, while my lover, on his knees, was motionless, passionately contemplating this libidinous spectacle. He saw, so he told me afterwards, his arrow as if in a sheath, appear and then disappear completely in its quiver.

After some moments of this delicious manoeuvre, my lover regained his strength and I felt the growing thickness of his member and inarticulate words came from his mouth. I warned him that I was once more ready to come and at the same moment a fresh jet of semen erupted and made us both nearly swoon with joy.

My well beloved Formatey had been in the right – I did take pleasure in it! How many times since, while bending over me, has he said:

'Watch out here it comes!'

More Erotica from Headline:

Lena's Story

Anonymous

**The Adventures of
a Parisian
Queen of the Night**

Irene was once a dutiful wife. Until, forsaking the protection of her husband, she embarked on a career as a sensuous woman: Lena, the most sought-after mistress in *fin de siècle* Paris. Yet despite the luxury, the champagne and the lavish attentions of her lovers, Lena feels her life is incomplete. She still longs for the one love that can satisfy her, the erotic pinnacle of a life of unbridled pleasure . . .

More titillating erotica available from Headline

Eros in the Country	Sweet Fanny
Eros in Town	The Love Pagoda
Eros on the Grand Tour	The Education of a Maiden
Venus in Paris	Maid's Night In
A Lady of Quality	

FICTION/EROTICA   0 7472 3334 9   £2.99